THE WHEAL ELIZA MURDER

By

C.R. Woollands

The Wheal Eliza Murder

The Wheal Eliza Murder © 2011 by C. R. Woollands

ISBN:

Publisher: OffTheBookShelf.com

Editor: Roxane Christ
www.aribert-editinghouse.com

C. R. Woollands

**I dedicate this book to my wife, Rachel.
You are my rock and guiding star.**

Acknowledgments

I would like to thank:

Mr. Roger Burton, author of *The Heritage of Exmoor* and *Simonsbath – The inside story of an Exmoor Village*, the people at the Barnstable Records' Office, the Somerset Records' Office and the Taunton local studies library for their help with my research.

My wife, Rachel, my children, Chad and Robert, who at the time of writing and researching for this book, have put up with travelling to and from Somerset and Devon.

My youngest son, Harry, who sat by my side, while writing the book.

My editor, Roxane Christ, who has stuck with me through thick and thin and opened my eyes to the art of writing.

C. R. Woollands

Introduction

Although I've always lived in Oxford, I have been drawn to the West Country ever since I was a child. I had grandparents in Bristol and relatives in Wales and Devon, so when we went on holidays, it was usually to that area. Now with a family of my own, we still visit the West Country and it was on one such visit to Ilfracombe in 2000 that I came across a book called '*Murder and Mystery in Exmoor*, by Jack Hurley. His book contained thirteen accounts of Murder and Mystery. The fourth, entitled '*A Shroud for Little Anna*,' took my interest. Upon looking further into the account and through my own research, I found the basis for the story. Over the years there have been many books written about the murder of Anna Maria Burgess in 1858, but none, to my knowledge, relating the story as it truly evolved.

The tale of this murder was recounted in the memoirs of Reverend William Thornton, who, in 1897, some forty years after the incident, wrote '*Reminiscences and Reflections of an Old West Country Clergyman*' (and we all know how the memory can play tricks). He wrote it in a way that made him, Thornton, the principal protagonist who hunted Burgess down and who took control in finding Anna's body. In truth, he was involved, yes, but not as he remembered it. Using the old records and the newspaper reports from *North Devon Journal* and *The Taunton Courier*, **The Wheal Eliza Murder** takes an in-depth look at not only Anna and William Burgess, but at Burgess's nemesis, the Rev. William Thornton, the investigation by Chief Superintendent Cresant Jeffs, the hunt for the murderer after he absconded to Wales and the seemingly endless search for Anna's body, the trial, the sentencing and finally the execution of the culprit.

The Wheal Eliza Murder relates the true facts behind the murder, the brutal slaying and disposal of the innocent six-year-old.

5

The Wheal Eliza Murder

It has taken me many years of research; visiting the remains of the
mine where William Burgess once worked and the second resting
place of Anna's body, the village where she grew up, and the
remains of the cottage she once called home.

Chapter One

Exmoor is "the moor where the River Exe rises". The Royal Forest of Exmoor, the central area is Simonsbath, known as Exmoor Forest, is the property of the Crown and a Royal Forest used for hunting and grazing.

The River Barle, which meanders over this barren land, is the largest river in the region even though the Exe gives its name to Exmoor and runs through the Barle Valley.

The Barle Valley was covered with snow. It had been a cold winter and today, February 7th 1857, was no exception. Today was the day they would bury Jane Burgess at St Andrews Church in Withypool. The forty-one-year-old woman had not succumb to, what the local's expected, at the hands of her husband, William, who was prone to violence when under the influence of strong drink. Measles was the cause of the poor woman's demise. Measles is a common ailment, which wouldn't have affected anyone else much, but combined with a lung inflammation and the woman's feeble constitution, within a week, it killed Jane Burgess.

William Burgess, at this time of his life was forty-one years old, and although he was a mild-looking man, of average height and light complexion with blue eyes, light brown hair and short bushy whiskers, he was a spirit of reckless determination and cruelty, and there was a complete absence of that pleasing look of intelligence in him. It was been frequently said, had not been able to boast a single friend in the world for the last thirty years; and, if true, this remark would seem to furnish a clue to the vicious and dissolute character of his early youth. He had little schooling as he could neither read or write; and his knowledge of the means of grace was too much like that of thousands of his class. The Parish church was merely appreciated as a "place to get married at". Before he was in his teens he was engaged in agricultural operations, or rather, employed to tend some of the stock, which, at that time, ranged the wilds of Exmoor Forest. Meanwhile, his behaviour and ungovernable ebullitions of temper were strongly marked, that his employer was at times to tell him "if you do not take care; you'll come some day to end your life on the gallows". As he grew up towards manhood, he worked for various farmers in the neighbourhood, and earned pretty good wages for a man of his kind. However, his besetting sin was the intoxicating cup, the "liquid rock" on which the lifeboat of many an English peasant had been wrecked and it was doubtless this sad propensity for drink, which the ignorant man indulged, that ultimately paved his path to the condemned cell.

Jane Shapland appeared to have been a person of careful and thrifty habits, and a kind and good mother to the little family that was now growing up around them. The genial influence of Jane was no doubt instrumental in keeping William from some of those excesses to which he was naturally prone. By indentation of economy and careful management, they got a few things about them, and everything appeared to foretell favourably for a happy future.

An outbreak of dissipation, however, drove William to resolve to emigrate to America. With this view, William's little stock of worldly goods was sold off, and he left Exmoor for Bristol, where he was born, where he was to look out for a berth in some emigrant ship. Upon reaching the United States, he was to send for Jane and his children. Instead of taking his passage to America, William started on a wild tour of profligacy. He went over to Wales, and there he remained drinking in many a public house, until his purse was lightened of a good portion of the money he possessed.

Returning home, William re-purchased some of the goods he had sold, and, to use his own words, "after this, they rubbed along pretty comfortably together". He again indulged in the excessive use of strong drink; and gradually his cup of domestic misery was filled to overflowing; that's when Jane caught the measles.

Jane had been married to William for nineteen years. Within that time they had five children, three daughters – the eldest, Mary, 16, Jane, 15, and the youngest, Anna, 6 – and two sons, Charles, 10 and John, 12. Although Jane was a good mother, she was an adulteress, with whom William profited thereby, which probably was disposed on drink. Three years before she married William at Exford in 1838, she gave birth to an illegitimate son, called Matthew, who was brought up by relatives at South Hill Farm in Withypool, where William's eldest, Mary, had been put into service.

The Wheal Eliza Murder

Chapter Two

The snow had stopped falling, but the ground was thick with the white of winter. Since the gravediggers knew they would have had a hard time, digging the frozen ground, they had dug Jane's resting place before morn's early rays.

William Burgess, his four children and some relatives were standing around the graveside. The Reverend Joseph Jeyko stood over the grave as he watched William cast some soil into the hole.

"Ashes to ashes, dust to dust," said the Reverend, as the soil scattered over the wooden box below.

Burgess looked down dispassionately at the coffin in the ground. Not once did he say anything and not once did a tear fall from him. His eldest, Mary, a strong country girl, stood apart from him, but near enough to comfort her siblings. Then, as if he was about to say something, the apparently forlorn father, turned, and with his family walked away. A group of funeral guests move to one side as he and his family made their way out of the churchyard. As they pass through the gate, Mary left her family and waited for another group of people to leave. She joined them and they walk off in the opposite direction.

Back at the graveside a small group of mourners, two women and two men, watch as Burgess walked away. The eldest woman turns to the others and said, "Let's see how he copes; now she's dead."

The younger woman replied, "I'm surprised she lasted as long as she did. Four Children and a husband who wastes his money on drink."

The eldest man moved in closer and said, "Rumour 'as it 'e killed her."

The younger woman turned to him sharply.

"Where'd you hear that? In the pub, I expect. Burgess may be a drunk and a waste of space, but he ain't no killer."

The older woman nodded. "That's right. Doctor said it was measles. He's not going to cope with those children."

"Well, he'd better sort something out soon," added the younger woman.

The gravediggers start to fill in the grave while the small group walked off.

A few days later at their home at Slate Quarry cottage in the Barle valley, Burgess came out of the cottage with three children. As he shut the door, his Daughter, Jane, tugged on his sleeve.

"Father! Reverend Thornton's coming," she cried.

Burgess turned and watched Rev. Thornton riding up to the cottage and getting off his horse. The Reverend William H. Thornton, a twenty-seven-year-old clergyman, had moved to Simonsbath a short while ago as the area's first minister, from the curacy of Lynton and Lynmouth, along with Countisbury, for which he held sole responsibility.

"Good morning, William, have I caught you at a bad time?" the Reverend asked.

"I am taking Charlie and Little Jane to North Molton," Burgess replied nervously.

"North Molton? Can I ask why? Thornton asked a bit puzzled.

"They're go' in to service."

"What about Anna?"

Burgess looked down at Anna his youngest daughter. Anna, a beautiful looking girl, with short brown hair, looked up at her father, as she clung to his leg.

"She'll be staying with me."

"I see. Is there anything I can do?"

Looking back up to Thornton, he replied, "I will have to find new lodgings; I can't afford the rent on the cottage anymore."

"I will see what I can do," Thornton said, shaking his head. "I'm sorry about your wife, William. I just got back from London.

Visiting my mother. She's ill, not long for this world I'm afraid, and got back to hear the news. How did it happen?"

Burgess lowered his head. "Measles," he replied sheepishly.

"Oh. I see. I'm sorry. Well, I'll keep in touch," Thornton said as he climbed back on his horse.

"Thank you, sir," Burgess answered as he turned away and walked off with his children. Thornton watched them for a while, then turned his horse and rode off.

Although Burgess had told Reverend Thornton that Anna was staying with him, after he had put Charles and Jane into service, he shortly placed her with a kind-hearted blacksmith, John Steer, and his family. John Steer's wife kept her and attended to her as one of her own children; and Anna's winsome and affectionate ways while in the family, won for her many friends; and when, for some reason or other she was taken away by Burgess, nearly a year later in January 1858, the Steers parted with her with much reluctance and regret.

Why he did this, nobody knew, but he took her to a farmhouse, which belonged to John Hayes, who was a relation of Burgess's wife, Jane and to where Burgess's eldest daughter, Mary and Jane's illegitimate son, Matthew, were already in service.

On Wednesday, the 13th of January, Burgess and Anna walked onto the farm and up to the farmhouse. Burgess eagerly knocked on the door and in a short while, the door opened. An elderly man of seventy-three-years of age stood in the doorway. He looked at Burgess with dislike in his face, but spoke to him civilly.

"Good day, Will. What can I do for you?"

Nervously, Burgess said, "John! I'm in a bit of a struggle."

"When aren't you?" John replied.

"Not always."

Changing the subject, John asked, "What do you want?"

"I've put Jane and Charlie, into service, and I need to put little Anna somewhere and I was hoping you'd take her in."

"I can't," John replied dryly.

"Why not?"

"I've got a houseful. Sarah, James's wife, is expecting and I have two of yours already."

"Surely you can..."

"I haven't the room. I've got Grace and Jane's child, Matthew and your Mary and John here and I've got no more room."

"Huh, I thought being family you'd help."

"*You're not family*!" John exploded angrily.

Burgess looked shocked.

Hayes returned the glare and added, "You're just Jane's useless husband."

Burgess was visibly getting irate. "I'll remember you said that."

"You do," John replied, stepping inside and slamming the door shut.

"I'll get you for that," Burgess shouted at the door.

Then looking down at Anna, he said in a quieter voice, "Come on. Let's go."

As father and daughter walked away, Anna looked up at Burgess and said, "He didn't mean it, Father."

"Yes, he did," Burgess replied, and then turning to the farmhouse, he shouted, "I'll teach you. You wait and see."

That night at the Hayes farm, William Burgess entered the farmyard and walked into the barn. He took down a lantern hanging from a hook, gave it a shake.

There was liquid in it. He then walked over to a stack of hay and grabbed a bundle. He dragged it out of the barn, and to the farmhouse. He took a knife out of his pocket and cut the twine from around the bundle. He then replaced the knife in his pocket and spread the hay across the doorway. With the devil's smile crossing his lips, Burgess opened the lantern and poured the liquid over the hay. He struck a match and threw it on the hay.

Within a moment, the hay erupted in flames as Burgess ran off into the night. He didn't turn to watch the fire eating its way up the door, spreading along the front of the house and climbing up to the windows, smashing them under the heat.

Meanwhile, the flames made their way quickly to the front room, caught hold of the chairs, table, and curtains – in minutes the farmhouse was ablaze.

From the edge of the farmyard, within the cover of some trees, Burgess stood in the darkness and eagerly watched his evil deed taking hold of John Hayes's abode.

Burgess laughed and said, "That'll teach you."

The next morning, John Hayes's son, James, a thirty-year-old farmer, like his father before him, was sitting outside the burnt remains of the farmhouse, comforting his thirty-five-year-old pregnant wife, Sarah and Mary Burgess. They looked at the farmhouse where James's seventy-two-year-old mother, Mary, was kneeling over the remains of three bodies; his father's, the one of the twenty-two-year-old, Matthew Shapland, and the one of the twelve-year-old, Grace Shapland, all covered in blankets.

Mary Burgess looked up at James and asked, "How did this happen?"

"Someone did this deliberately and I've got my suspicions who," James replied.

"Who do you think done this?" she asked again.

James looked at her with hate in his eyes and said, "Never you mind. He'll pay."

A few months later, Burgess was now living with a woman called Jane Ford. He had kept his nose clean and kept out of trouble, apparently.

We know nothing of Jane Ford. Where she lived, no one mentioned her even in passing. The only time she is mentioned is at his trial, in a deposition given by William Smith, a boot maker and publican in North Molton. However, and even though Burgess was keeping out of trouble, trouble was looming elsewhere in the county.

In the vicarage next to St. Luke's Church in Simonsbath, the thirty-one-year-old wife of Reverend Thornton, Grace, was lying in bed in her bedroom. With her was Ms. Emma Reed. Emma was in her early twenties and two other women in their forties. Grace Thornton was in the process of giving birth to her first child.

"Push, Grace. Push," Emma said to Grace while one of the other women was wiping Grace's brow. "Come on," Emma said again, "Push. I can see its head."

"I can't," Grace cried. "Where's the doctor?"

"Someone's gone to get him, dear. Now, push," said the woman, wiping her brow.

Emma knelt closer and said, "Push, Grace."

Downstairs in the living room, Reverend Thornton was pacing about the room as a man in his forties stood by the door, watching him.

"Why hasn't the doctor come yet?" Thornton asked impatiently.

"This be the trouble, sir," replied the man, "one doctor for the whole parish."

Thornton stopped pacing and looked at the man, "But he knows she due now and young Kingdom should have reached him and been back by now."

"That he would have, sir," the man answered, "But the doctor could be somewhere else. But don't worry; Bess has experience with delivering babies."

"Yes, you have a good woman there, Tom," Thornton replied.

Back upstairs, Bess, Tom's wife, was kneeling in front of Grace, while Emma was now wiping Grace's brow.

"It's coming, dear," she said. "Push a bit harder."

Grace pushed harder.

"Nearly there, Grace," Emma said.

"One more push," Bess called out.

Grace pushed, screamed and then relaxed as Bess held the baby up.

"Well done, dear," she burst out, with joy in her smile. "You have a baby girl."

"Well done, Grace," Emma rejoined, as Bess smacked the baby's bottom. The newborn wailed for the entire house to hear.

Downstairs, Rev. Thornton heard his daughter's first cry too.

"There you go, sir," Tom said, smiling at the new father.

Not waiting for another comment, Rev. Thornton ran out of the room and up the stairs. Tom followed.

In the bedroom, as Bess was wrapping the baby in a shawl, the little girl suddenly stopped crying.

"Oh no!" Bess cried out.

"What is it?" Grace asked.

Bess looked at Grace ruefully, saying, "I'm sorry, my dear, she's dead."

Grace looked at her with disbelief and then screamed out, "Nooo!"

"Dead? How?" Emma asked.

"No, she can't be, she was just crying," Grace shouted, wriggling in the midst of despair in her bed.

Bess laid the baby down and replied, "She wasn't strong enough."

Grace screamed again, "Nooo!" as Rev. Thornton burst through the door.

"What is it? Where is it?" he asked, looking at everyone in turn. "What's the matter?"

"I'm sorry, William," Emma replied, lowering her gaze, "Your daughter didn't make it."

"What... Daughter... But ... I heard her," Thornton blurted uncomprehendingly.

"Yes. But she wasn't strong enough to carry on," Bess answered, shaking her head.

Rev. Thornton walked over to Grace, knelt down next to her, taking his wife's hand into both of his.

"I'm sorry," he said meaningfully.

"We had a daughter," Grace told him simply.

"Don't worry, dear," Bess said, as she pulled the blanket over the baby, "You're young. You have plenty of time to try again."

"Yes, Bess is right. We have plenty of time," Thornton whispered, caressing his wife's forehead.

Unexpectedly, Grace grabbed hold of her husband's hand. He looked up at her and she said, "I want to get out of this place," sternly.

"Of course. It's understandable with what's happened. But rest now and we'll talk about it later," he said blandly as he turned round to look at the other women.

"Leave her please. Let her rest," he added after a pause.

Taking with them the bedclothes and linen, the three women left the room without a word.

Later that day, Rev. Thornton entered the dark bedroom, carrying a tray with cups and a teapot on it. He walked over to the table, placed the tray down, pulled open the curtains and looked over at the bed. He picked the tray up and walked over to the bed, placed it over the cover and sat next to his wife.

Grace opened her eyes, when she heard her husband moving about the room, she looked up at him.

"How are you feeling?" he asked.

"Terrible," Grace replied softly. "William, I do want to get out of this place."

"Yes. I was thinking about that," Thornton said as he got up from the bed and walked slowly across the room. "What you need is a break away and recover your strength." He stopped by the window and turned to her and asked, "Why don't you go and visit your father," concern tainting his voice.

Sitting up, and pushing the tray out of the way, Grace replied, "Yes, I will. But I want to move from here altogether."

"But this is my parish. I can't just up and leave," Thornton erupted, walking back to the bed.

"I know. But this barren land will bring no good."

"Look. While you're away, I will have a talk to Mr. Knight and see what he can suggest," Thornton said, placating.

"All right, that's a start," Grace replied with a smile.

"Good. Now have some tea." Thornton sat down on the bed and poured Grace a cup of tea while no more words were exchanged about the whole affair.

Chapter Three

On the night of Sunday, the 30th of May, in the village of North Molton, Burgess was walking along the dark road to the public house called 'The Swan Inn', when he looked up at the sign, which was gently swinging in the wind. He looked around him and then went in.

Inside, the open fire burned brightly in the hearth. In the corner, a man was singing folk songs to the inebriated patrons. A fiddler and a man, playing a penny whistle, accompanied him in his rhythmic sing-along.

The fifty-two-year-old landlord, William Smith, was serving a customer as the door to the pub opened. Smith looked up and saw Burgess walk in. As he walked to the bar, smiling and tapping people on the shoulder, the landlord called to him.

"Evening Will!"

Burgess looked over at him, somewhat deprecatingly.

"Evening! Give us some ale," he ordered as he pointed to an empty table in the corner.

The landlord nodded while Burgess made his way to the corner and sat down. Not a minute later the pub owner came to the table, deposited a large jug of ale in front of the patron, poured him a glassful, grumbled something inaudible and walked away.

"And some food when you've got time," Burgess called after Smith.

The landlord waved a hand acknowledging the order, as he reached the bar.

Burgess drank the ale down fast, lets out a burp, and sat the glass down with a thud. He poured himself another glass and emptied the jug with the third. Smashing the glass down he yelled, "And another ale!"

"I've only one pair of hands," shouted Smith, already annoyed.

Burgess sat impatiently for a while, waiting for his food and ale refills. Since his first jug of ale had not quenched his thirst, he would need much more before the night was done.

Eventually Smith walked over with a jug and as he poured the ale into Burgess's glass, he asked, "You coming to the club, tomorrow night?"

"Yes. Should be a good night," Burgess replied.

Having no time to make conversation, Smith walked off back to the bar.

While Burgess swallowed another mouthful of ale, he shouted to Smith, "I need to talk to you about some boots."

Smith stopped and turned around abruptly. "Buying or selling?"

"Buying," Burgess grumbled his mouth full of meat.

Interested, Smith walked back to the table and sat down opposite his patron.

"For yourself?" he asked.

"No. Little 'un."

"Okay. Bring her by and I'll get her measured."

"Okay. Um. How much they cost?

Getting up, Smith replied, "For you, ninepence."

"And for anybody else?" Burgess asked.

Smith looked down, smiled and replied, "Ninepence."

Burgess nodded and while he returned to his hearty chewing and drinking, Smith walked back to the bar.

As the din among the patrons got louder, Burgess carried on with his drinking.

Two weeks later, on the 14th of June, in the Cobbler's shop, which was situated opposite the Swan Inn public house. It was also owned and run by William Smith. Burgess stormed into the shop, shouting, "Smith! Smith! Where are you?"

A young man, in his early twenties, jumped up from behind the counter, when he heard the shouts. "Yes, can I help you?" he asked.

"Not you. Your father," Burgess said.

"I'll get him," replied the young man, scurrying to the back of the shop.

A minute later, he re-entered the shop with his father.

"Ah, Burgess!" William Smith said, "Come to settle up for the boots?"

"I've come for the boots, settling up's another matter," Burgess replied angrily.

"What's wrong with the boots?" Smith senior asked.

"What's wrong? I haven't got them yet, that's what's wrong."

"I sent them out over a week ago, to where you're staying with that Ford woman."

"She say's they ain't been sent," Burgess replied, getting more aggravated by the minute.

"I took them myself," Smith junior said. "That woman came in with the little girl, two weeks ago. I measured her up, made up the boots and took them myself to her cottage. She said you'd stop by and pay up."

"Well, I ain't got them. She said they ain't been sent. So someone's lying."

"Well, it's not us," Smith senior replied, visibly offended. "You'd better sort it out with that woman."

"I'll sort it out, don't you worry none!"

"You still need to pay ninepence," Smith senior insisted.

"I'll pay it, when I get the boots!"

Burgess shot an angry glance at both men, then turned and left the shop, slamming the door shut after him.

"You know you're not going to see either him or the money," Smith junior said, looking into the face of his worried father.

"I know," replied his father.

"What do you think happened to the boots?"

"He's got them."

"So why come here and rant on?"

"Because he expected me to bow down to his ranting and make him another pair," Smith senior said as he walked to the front door.

"Do you really think that's what he had in mind?"

Smith senior turned away from the door, and said, "Knowing Will Burgess as well as I do, that's exactly what he had in mind."

The Red Deer Inn, by which name it was known by most of the locals until 1843, was now nicknamed, The Gallon House. The reason the inn was called the Gallon House was that nothing less than a gallon of ale was served to its patrons then.

On the 22nd of June, a week later, the door of the inn opened and Burgess stood in the doorway. He looked into the bar and then down to his side at Anna.

"Sit there and don't move," he told her, pointing to the front step.

Anna sat on the step obediently as Burgess shut the door and walked to the bar. As he reached the bar, the proprietor, James Mills, a sixty-four-year-old, walked up to him. He looked at Burgess and nodded.

Burgess returned the gaze and said, "Some ale!"

Mills reached over and grabbed a big jug, poured out some ale into a glass and handed it to Burgess. He took a couple of gulps, placed the glass on the counter and said, "James! Is there any room over the road for me and my little Anna?"

"Probably," James answered. "You'll have to see Mrs. Marley, if she's got room."

"Okay right, I'll ask."

"You still working, Will?" asked James.

"Yeap."

Mills nodded. "Well, finish your drink and go and see her."

"Thanks," replied Burgess.

He finished the ale, put down the glass and walked to the door.

Within half an hour, the bedroom door opened. Father and daughter had found themselves a room. Mrs. Sarah Marley, a thirty-seven-year-old portly woman, entered the room first, followed by Burgess and Anna. Burgess looked unimpressed.

The room was shabby and smelled of mildew. The dirty curtains hung askew. The bed linen was grimy and grey and the washstand looked as if it had never been wiped with soap or water for ages. *'Beggars can't be choosers,'* Burgess thought.

Mrs. Marley turned to them and said, without any excuse in her voice, "This is it. Not much, but for two shillings and six pence a week, what do you expect?"

"That's all right," Burgess replied.

"Good. You know me, Will Burgess; I don't tolerate fighting or loud noise at night, and there are other people who live here."

"That'll be fine," he said reluctantly – knowing full well that on some occasions, he would wake the whole village if he'd been drinking his fill.

"When do you want it from?" she asked.

"Now."

"Until when?"

"Don't know."

She walked over to the window, brushed the curtain and asked, a nosing tone in her voice, "You still working?"

"Yes."

"Where?"

"At the mine on the moors."

Mrs. Marley walked back over to them and said, with a reassured smile, "That's alright then. You'll be sharing this room with someone else that works there."

"Who?" Burgess asked, raising an eyebrow.

"William Cockram," she replied. "You know him?"

"Yes."

"Do you get on?"

"Yes."

"That's all right then. I don't want you fighting in here."

"There won't be."

"Good."

Mrs. Marley then left the room and shut the door.

Burgess put his bag down and looked at his little girl.

"How long do we have to stay here for, Father?" Anna asked, twisting her fingers in front of her.

"Shut your whining, child," he shouted, but then looking down at her again, with a quieter voice, he said, "I don't know how long."

"I miss Mother," Anna remarked, going to sit on the bed.

"Yes, I know, and I miss her too." Burgess couldn't help but feel sorry and concerned for his child. He went to kneel beside her, surrounding her frail body with his strong arms.

Just over a week later, while workers at the mine were leaving for the day, Burgess and William Cockram, a strapping young man of twenty-five-years, who worked down in the mines, while Burgess worked on the surface, left work together and walked over the moor, towards home. As they entered the front door, Mrs. Marley walked out of the living room and stopped Burgess.

"I want a word with you," she demanded.

Cockram shot a glance at Burgess and walked upstairs, saying nothing.

"You owe me half a crown for last week's rent," she continued.

"You'll get it," Burgess answered. "I'm a bit short of money at the moment."

"You wouldn't be if you didn't spend it on drink. You've got a child to care for as well," she protested.

"You'll get it."

"I'd better get it soon or you and the child are out!"

Burgess brushed past Mrs. Marley and walked up the stairs – he was fuming.

Mrs. Marley watched as he went up and when he was out of sight, she returned to the living room, shrugging her shoulders.

As Burgess entered the bedroom, he found Cockram sitting on the bed with Anna – she was showing him a little doll. Anna jumped from the bed and running to her father, she said, "Hello, Father," happily throwing her arms around his legs.

"You're costing me a fortune, my girl," he said, caressing her hair.

Her smile disappeared while she returned to the bed and grabbed her doll ruefully.

"Isn't there any of your family that could take her in?" Cockram asked, seeing the hurt painted on Anna's face. "It will cut your rent down a bit."

"I've got a sister in Porlock, but I doubt they could have her. They've only got a small place. And every one else, has my other children, they won't take any more," Burgess replied, shrugging.

"Have you asked your sister?" Cockram asked.

"No."

Cockram got up from the bed and walked over to Burgess. "Well how do you know if you don't ask?"

Burgess nodded. "I'll go and see her at the weekend."

Picking Anna up from the bed, Cockram held her in his arms and she played with the dolls hair.

"If they do have her, then you won't be charged a high rent."

Burgess looked at Anna, who smiled back at him.

"As I said, I can ask, but I doubt they will."

A couple of days later, as the morning light shone through the curtains, Cockram woke up, stretched, pushed back the covers and stood up. He looked down at the bed and saw Burgess and Anna still there.

Cockram called down to him, "Will! Will! Wake up."

Burgess stirred; his eyes not eagerly willing to open properly as he saw the daylight come through the curtains.

"W... Wh...What time is it?" he asked his voice groggy with sleep.

Cockram took his watch chain from the bedpost.

"Eight o'clock," he replied. "I thought you were going to your sister's?"

Burgess sat up. "Eight o'clock in the morning? Damn, I overslept." He lay back down. "I'll have to go next week."

"That's another half a crown you got to give her," Cockram said.

"I know," Burgess replied and went back to sleep.

The Wheal Eliza Murder

Chapter Four

On Saturday, the 24th of July, outside the Gallon House cottage, Anna was playing as Mrs. Marley was washing some clothes in a tin tub, with two of Mrs. Marley's daughters, Sarah and Emma. Mrs. Marley's youngest child, Mary, was sitting next to her mother. Burgess walked out of the building, walked up to Mrs. Marley and sat down on a pile of logs, next to where she was working.

"I'm taking the maid to her Aunt's in Porlock in the morning; can you get her cleaned and get some clothes ready?" he said to her.

"What time are you leaving?"

"About six."

"How long will she be gone?"

Burgess looked at Anna playing with the other children. "I don't know."

"Okay," Mrs. Marley replied, "once I've finished this, I'll get her things ready."

"Thanks."

"You'll not be staying with your sister then?" Mrs. Marley asked.

"No. Ain't no room. I'll be back by tomorrow night."

Mrs. Marley turned her gaze to the little girl. She was a compassionate woman, but she could not afford to have Anna stay without her father pay for her fare – Times were hard for everyone. "Going to be quiet here without her."

"I know," he said, bowing his head ruefully.

As he looked at his daughter again, she stopped, turned to her father, smiled and waved at him. Burgess waved back, got up and walked inside.

The next morning, Burgess was getting dressed when Cockram stirred in the bed. Cockram sat up, looked at Burgess, who asked, "William! Will you please tell me what time it is?"

"Pass me my watch then," Cockram said.

Burgess walked over to the end of the bed, picked up the watch hanging on the post and handed it to Cockram. Cockram struggled to see the time in the little light there was and replied, "Half past three."

"Are you going to your sister's?" he asked.

"Yes."

Cockram nodded and lay back down again.

Burgess finished dressing, walked over to Anna, and gave her a gentle shove.

"Anna, come, turn out," he whispered.

Anna sat up, rubbed her eyes, got out of bed and got dressed. Burgess picked up a bag; they left the room and made their way downstairs.

As they stood outside the cottage in the dark, Burgess pulled up the collar of his coat. The rain was pouring down hard by then.

"Can't we wait until it stops raining?" Anna asked, looking up at her father pleadingly.

"No. We go now," Burgess said and walked over the road.

Instead of turning right, as he left the cottage to go along the road, which would take them to Porlock, he crossed the road and walked alongside the Gallon House Inn, around the back and across the rough moor lands on Red Stone Hill.

They walked farther over the moor, eventually the Gallon House was out of sight.

"Is it far?" asked Anna.

"Keep your mouth shut," Burgess shouted. He stopped, turned to Anna, knelt down in front of her. "Anna! Since your mother died, we've struggle to get by."

"Yes, Father," Anna replied.

"And at the moment we are struggling the hardest."

Anna looked up at him.

"We're not going to Porlock, because Auntie Betty and Uncle John have no room there," he said.

"Why did we leave Mrs. Marley's?"

"Because I couldn't afford the two of us staying there," Burgess confessed.

"Where are we going then?"

"You'll be going somewhere safe and peaceful," Burgess told her.

"Me? Where will you be staying?"

"At Mrs. Marley's. Come here, child."

Anna moved closer to Burgess. He hugged her and said, "I do love you. You do know that, don't you?"

"Yes, Father," she said, wrapping her arms around his neck.

Burgess released her, placed his hands on her shoulders and looked into her eyes. He saw Anna smile at him. Burgess smiled back, "Come on let's go."

Anna turned and walked on. Burgess watched her walk off and as he started to stand up; he saw a big stick lying on the ground. He picked it up, stood up and walked after Anna, using the stick as a walking cane.

Porlock is a picturesque village situated on the North Coast of Exmoor. The wooded slopes flank the seaside village and are below a 1-in-4 radiant hill with hairpin bends. At that time, tourists to West Somerset and North Devon, arriving in carriages, had to get out and walk up the hill. The hills of Exmoor surround Porlock on three sides, with the heather covered moors cut by deep, often wooded Combes with clear sparkling streams at their base. Porlock Weir is only two miles away and is a quaint little harbour with a unique charm that has to be experienced. Occasionally, at very low tide, remains of a prehistoric forest can be seen.

In between Porlock village and Porlock Weir is a road called West Porlock, and at number 46, lived the Moore family. John Moore, a burly fifty-four-year-old man and his thirty-eight-year-old wife, Betty, Burgess's sister, with their three daughters, fourteen-year-old, Faith, twelve-year-old, Betty, and seven-year-old, Mary, was the family that William was on his way to visit. In fact, this was where Anna was supposed to stay – that's what he had told Mrs. Marley.

Just before seven in the morning, Burgess was walking along West Porlock. The rain was still pouring down, but it did not deter Burgess from making his way to his sister's house.

It was still raining, when Burgess walked up to the backdoor and knocked.

After a short time, the window upstairs opened and a woman looked out.

"Yes? Who is it?" she asked.

Burgess looked up and replied, "It's me, Betty. William."

"Do you know what time it is?" she asked.

"Sorry. I...," Burgess started to say.

"I will be down in a minute," she called. She popped her head back in, shut the window, and a few minutes later, she opened the door and let him in.

"Will!" she said, "What a surprise. Come in. You must be drenched."

Burgess silently walked in and the woman shut the door.

"Take your coat off, I'll hang it to dry," Betty told him.

Burgess remained silent, put down the bag and took his coat and leggings off.

Faith, Betty's oldest daughter, entered the room, curious to see who the early visitor was. Betty turned to her and said, "Light the fire, will you, please."

"Yes, Mother," the young girl replied as she knelt down by the fireplace and started to place wood and paper in the hearth.

Burgess handed his sister his coat and leggings and as Betty hung the coat up, she told him to sit down. He did as bidden and stretched his hands over the newly lit fire.

John Moore came down the stairs and strode into the room, adjusting his braces over his shirt. He looked at Burgess and said, "Will Burgess! Who's after you now?"

"No one," Burgess replied, evading John's gaze.

"We're going to have breakfast. Do you want some?" Betty asked.

"I wouldn't say no," Burgess answered.

"Thought not," John said, as he sat down.

"John!" Betty shouted.

Betty started to prepare breakfast as the children appeared, sat down at the table and looked strangely at the man sitting beside them.

Betty looked at the girls and said, "Say hello to your Uncle William, girls."

Little Betty and her Sister, Mary, looked at him and together, they replied, "Good morning, Uncle William."

Burgess was still watching John nervously. He looked away from John to the girls and with a smile on his face, he replied, "Good morning, girls."

John, eying Burgess suspiciously, asked, "So. What's the matter?"

Spooked by the question, Burgess replied, "Nothing."

John, even more suspicious, sat back in his chair. "Come off it. You don't usually show up. Stealing sheep again?"

"I've done nothing. Nobody is after me; I just got restless during the night and went for a walk."

"And ended up here?" John questioned, raising an eyebrow.
"Yes!"

John looked at Burgess in disbelief, shaking his head slowly as Betty placed a plate of bacon in front of him and Burgess. There was bread on the table and a small plate of butter. He looked up at his wife and said, "Thanks, love."

"Yes," Burgess said as well to her. "Thanks. Looks great. I'm starved."

Burgess dug in heartily while John and the girls stared at him as he ate.

Betty looked round at them. "Girls!" she called. The girls looked away and John started his breakfast.

Betty got a pot of coffee off the stove and brought it to the table, where John picked it up and poured himself a cup. When he replaced it on the table; Burgess picked it up and poured himself a cup as well.

After eating his breakfast, Burgess sat back, patted his stomach and said, "That was great, Betty."

Still eating her breakfast, she swallowed what she had in her mouth, turned to him and replied, "Thank you."

John finished off his breakfast; put his knife and fork down on the empty plate, and looked at his wife. "Yes. Nice piece of bacon." Returning his attention to Burgess, he added, "So, come on, Will, why are you here?"

"I told you, I went for a walk," Burgess shouted.

"Don't shout in my house," John shouted back. "You may bully other people, but you don't scare me."

"I'm sorry," Burgess replied, quickly regaining his calm.

He looked at Betty and the girls, "I'm sorry for my outburst. But I am telling the truth." He looked back at John and added, "Why won't you believe me?"

"Because you're a man, who gets by, by lying and it's hard to know when you're telling the truth or not."

"I know. But I am telling the truth now. Nobody is after me."

"Okay," John answered, leaning back in his chair.

Betty looked at her husband and then at her brother and changed the subject.

"So where are you living now?"

"I'm staying at the Red Deer cottages."

"The where?" John interrupted.

"Red Deer cottages, opposite the Red Deer Inn."

"Never heard of it." John shook his head. "Then I haven't been up that way for a few years."

"Course you have," Burgess said. "The Gallon House Inn."

"Oh yes. Has it got new owners and changed the name?"

"No. It's been called that for years, but the locals still know it as the Gallon House."

"How are the children?" Betty cut-in, changing the subject again.

Burgess looked startled. He hesitated for a fraction of a second before answering. "They're okay. They went into service in North Molton. I couldn't look after them with my Jane gone."

"Yes. A fine Woman," Betty said, nodding.

"Yes, she was. Anyway, what's the time?" Burgess asked.

John took out his pocket watch and looked at it. "Nine thirty."

"Ah well, better go and walk this breakfast off," the brother-in-law said contentedly.

He and his sister stood up. Betty collected his coat and leggings, which had partially dried and handed it to him. He sat on a bench near the door and put them on.

Meanwhile, John and the girls were still sitting at the table. John, still not sure of the reason behind Burgess's visit, watched him eagerly. Ignoring his brother-in-law's stare, Burgess stood up and put his coat on.

Betty stood by the door and said to him, "Well! It was nice seeing you again."

Finally, John stood up and walked over to his wife. "Yes. Stop by anytime and please forgive me for asking questions."

Betty looked strangely at her husband as he held his hand out. Burgess looked at the hand, took hold of it and they both shook hands. He smiled. "That's alright, it's understandable."

Betty looked at her daughters and said, "Say goodbye to your uncle, girls."

All three of them stood up and at the same time replied, "Goodbye, Uncle William."

Burgess looked at them and answered with a smile, "Bye girls." He then looked at Betty and John and added, "Thanks for breakfast." He finished doing up his coat, picked up the bag, opened the door and turned back to Betty and John.

Betty looked at him curiously and said, "You take care and don't get too wet."

"I won't. Bye," Burgess replied and walked out into the rain.

Betty shut the door, turned to her husband and looked at him, bewilderment painted on her face.

"What was that all about?" she asked.

"He's in trouble, somewhere. I can tell you that much," her husband replied, shaking his head.

"Why do you always put him down?" Betty obviously wanted to believe that her brother had just been passing through.

"Because he's a no-hoper," John answered. "You've said it yourself, plenty of times. His wife put up with a lot with him. She's better off dead, than put up with him anymore."

"John!" Betty shouted at him, "The children. And she wasn't that pure as well."

John looked at his daughters, who had sat down again and were finishing off their breakfast, "You should know what he's like," he said to them, "A waste of space. He's done something. Something beyond what he's done before and he'll pay for it with his life. You mark my words." He turned back to his wife and asked, "What do you mean not pure?"

Betty grabbed hold of his arm, looked at the girls and said, "Finish your breakfast." Then she took John to the corner of the room and with a whisper, so the girls couldn't hear them, said to him, "She wasn't that good of a wife."

"What do you mean?" John asked, somewhat taken aback by his wife's remark. "She seemed okay by me. Too good for your brother."

"They've always struggled, with his drinking and she used to make up the money by..."

"By what?" John asked.

Reluctantly she whispered, "By whoring."

"No!" John shouted.

"Shhhh..." Betty hushed him, shooting a glimpse at their daughters.

John looked over at the girls, who were still eating, then back to Betty. He shook his head. "No. I can't believe it. She's always seemed the prim and proper woman."

"Well," Betty replied with a smug look on her face, "now you know."

Chapter Five

When Burgess arrived at the cottage, John Marley, the forty-eight-year-old husband of Sarah, was sitting on the step whittling a piece of wood to pass the time.

He looked up at Burgess and said, "Hello, Burgess. You're back early."

"Yes. I didn't want to bide my time there, long. The sister's husband doesn't like me much," Burgess replied. He then walked into the cottage. When he had gone inside, Marley continued to whittle and whispered, "I wonder why?"

That night, in the dark bedroom, Burgess was sleeping restlessly. He was tossing, turning and mumbling to himself. The door opened and Burgess sat up and shouted, "Anna!"

Cockram entered the room and was startled by Burgess's outburst. He looked at Burgess and replied, "No, Will. It's me. You okay?"

Burgess looked up at him blankly and replied, "Yes. I..., I just miss Anna."

Cockram shut the door and said, "She stayed at your sister's then."

"Yes."

Cockram walked over to the bed, sat on the edge and started to get undressed. "How long is she going to be staying there?" he asked.

"A while."

"Well, you'll see her now and again, won't you?" Cockram asked.

"I suppose so."

Cockram climbed into bed and as he settled to get comfortable, he said, "…and have a bit extra money in your pocket now.

Burgess lay back down, "Yes. That'll be nice," he replied, turned over and went back to sleep.

Cockram looked at Burgess, then shut his eyes and went to sleep.

The next night in the Red Deer Inn, two men, in their thirties, were sitting in the corner, huddled up together, talking. Both men were scruffy looking, but always had money for ale. The first man looked around him nervously as he whispered to his friend, "I've noticed a fresh mound, up on the hill side."

"So?" replied the second man.

"So, don't you see? Buried stolen sheep."

Nodding, the second man said, "I see."

"If we go up there and dig them up, we can put them safe somewhere and sell them later."

As the second man thought about what his friend said, Burgess walked into the pub. The first man looked up at him and shouted, "Will! Over here."

Burgess looked at the man, nodded and walked to the bar.

The first man whispered in his friend's ear, "Will can help us."

"What for?"

"God, you must be the stupidest person in the village."

"Hey! Watch what you're saying," the second man shouted.

The first man back-handed the second man on the arm and groaned, "Quiet, you idiot. Look, by the looks of the size of the mound, there could be a couple sheep buried there, so we will need help to carry them."

"If there's two sheep, we won't need Burgess. We can carry one each."

The first man placed his head into his hand and slowly shook it, not believing what he was hearing. Then in a calmer tone, he replied, "We've got to cut them up, while we're up there and we're going to need help. Trust me."

Burgess walked over to where the two men were sitting, carrying a glass of ale, sat down and said, "What's up?"

"We need some help," the first man whispered.

Knowing by the whisper it was something illegal, Burgess whispered back, "With what?"

"To get some buried sheep," replied the second man.

"Where?"

"On the moor about two miles north of here. There's a freshly dug deads," said the first man.

Looking shocked, Burgess replied cautiously, "Have you checked the deads?"

The first man shook his head and said, "No. I was getting some help and go up there tomorrow night and get them. You in?"

"Tomorrow night. What time?" Burgess asked.

"About elevenish. Are you in or not?" the first man demanded.

"Yes," Burgess replied.

The first man sat back in his chair and said, "Good. We'll meet up, outside here and make a big profit."

Burgess nodded, quickly drank his ale, put the empty glass down, got up and said, "Okay. I'll meet you then." He then turned around and walked out of the inn.

When he was gone, the second man asked, "Are you sure, you can trust him?"

"Course we can," replied his friend, "he's stolen more sheep from the deads before. He ain't going to tell."

James Mills, the landlord of the inn, watched Burgess leave and then looked over at the two men in the corner. He walked over to them and asked, "What have you said to Burgess?"

The men looked up at him and the first man said, "Nothing. Why?"

Mills peered at them with curiosity. "Well, it is very strange that William Burgess comes in here and leaves after one glass of ale."

"Yes, I thought that was odd," answered the second man, "Maybe he's got something on his mind."

Mills raised an eyebrow. "Yes, maybe. I wonder what?"

After resting his gaze for a moment on the two patrons once again, Mills then turned around and as he walked back to the bar, the first man shouted, "Can we have two more ales, James?"

Mills shouted without turning around, "In a minute, I've got other people to serve first."

The two men looked at each other and sat back in their chairs, relieved.

Chapter Six

The next day, as Burgess and Cockram walked up to the house after a hard day's work, Mrs. Marley was sitting on a stool by the door. Burgess noticed her as they neared the cottage.

"I bet she's after the rent," Burgess said.

"I ain't worried, I've got the rent. Have you?" Cockram replied.

"Yes. Now Anna's in Porlock."

"Got nothing to worry about then, have you?"

"No."

As they walked up to the door Mrs. Marley called out, "Will Burgess!"

Burgess stopped. Cockram looked at Mrs. Marley then at Burgess and walked into the cottage.

"I have the rent," Burgess said defiantly.

"That's good, but I want to ask you something."

"Go on."

"Are there any children where the little maid is, to play with?"

"Yes. Plenty."

"Is she going to be staying there long?"

"No."

Mrs. Marley hesitated and then said, "If you were to leave her with me, I would keep her and use her as a child of my own."

"She's happy with her family," Burgess replied.

"Yes. Well, if you change your mind...."

"I'll keep it in mind," Burgess said and walked into the cottage, leaving Mrs. Marley to her duties.

While Burgess was wandering the moors, the two men he had met at the inn the previous night were waiting for him outside the establishment. The inn was now closed and all the lights were out. The two men stumped their feet silently as the cold wind was piercing through their thin clothes. The second man looked knowingly at the first man and said, "I told you he wouldn't turn up."

"He will, let's give him a bit more time," replied his friend.

The second man pointed and said, "He's only staying over there. There's no lights on and it's the time you told him to be here. So where is he?"

"I don't know."

"Well are we going to do it on our own?"

"No. Too risky."

"What do you mean, too risky?"

"We don't want the chance of carrying too much of the carcass and somebody seeing us," answered the first man.

His friend shook his head. "Somebody could see us, even if Burgess was here."

"Yes, but then there'd be three of us, each carrying part of the carcass, it wouldn't be too noticeable than just two people carrying."

"What do you want to do then?"

The first man shrugged his shoulders. "Leave it for tonight and try tomorrow night."

"Are we going to find someone else to help us?"

"Yes."

"Well, make it someone you can really trust."

The first man agreed. They said good night to each other and walked off in opposite directions. When the first man was out of ear-shot, the second man said, "And he reckoned I was the stupidest bloke in the village. Now who looks foolish?"

In the darkness and quietness of a cold night, the first man walked along a track across the moor land of Hereliving, then Winstitchen and made his way along the ridge near the Wheal Eliza mine that had stopped work, due to it being unproductive since 1857.

He was walking along the hillside, when he heard someone walking by on a ridge below. He ducked down and cautiously looked, but couldn't see anyone.

The footsteps continued crunching the stony track below in the direction of the old disused mine, and progressively became soundless. Frustrated, the man got up and walked off towards Simonsbath.

Unbeknownst to him, the footsteps he heard belonged to the man, who was supposed to have met up with him and his friend, earlier that night – William Burgess.

The next morning, John Mills was walking across the field behind the inn when he came to a spot where a fire had been burning. He put his foot in the ash, breaking it up. The look on his face was one of bewilderment. He looked around, and then walked away pensively.

When he came back that way, that evening with his thirty-two-year-old brother, Edwin, they came to the spot where he had found the pile of ashes, the two men stopped and John said to his brother, "I noticed this here this morning."

"So," replied Edwin, "someone lit a fire here, to keep warm."

John picked up a stick and poked at the ash. He uncovered some buttons, hooks and eyes, a piece of fur and a piece of cloth. He picked up the cloth and said, "Someone's been burning clothes. Go down to the cottage and get one of the women up here."

"What for?" Edwin asked.

"Because, this cloth looks like it's from women's clothing and I want to see if any of them recognise it or know anything about it."

Edwin shrugged his shoulders and ran down the hill.

At the cottage, thirty-year-old, Mary Farley, Mrs. Marley's neighbour, was taking some clothes off the line, as Edwin ran up to her.

Out of breath, Edwin asked, "Mary! You haven't been burning any clothes in the field, have you?"

Shaking her head, she replied, "No. Why?"

"We found some burnt cloth. John reckons it's from women's clothing."

"I'll come and have a look."

Mary and Edwin ran back across the field, to where John was waiting. When they got to him, he handed Mary the piece of cloth and said, "Do you recognise it?"

Mary took it and looked at it closely, and after a few seconds replied, "Yes. I've seen this print before."

"Where?" John asked.

"At the cottage. I've seen Sarah wash something with that pattern on it."

"Does it belong to her?"

"No. I think it was little Anna Burgess's."

"Go and ask Sarah to have a look at it."

Mary didn't hesitate; turned on her heals and ran back to the cottage.

John looked back at the ashes on the ground and said, "Why burn the child's clothes."

Edwin shrugged his shoulders and replied, "I don't know."

Mary ran up to the back-door of the cottage, went inside and called out, "Sarah! Where are you?"

Sarah Marley answered from inside the pantry, "In here."

"Quick. Have a look at this."

Sarah came out of the pantry staring at Mary, a question mark on her face. "Look at what?"

Mary handed her the piece of cloth.

"This."

"It's a piece of burnt cloth!" Sarah was visibly confused.

"Yes. But do you recognise the print on it?"

Sarah looked closely at the cloth. "Yes. It looks like the print on Anna Burgess's pinafore."

"That's what I thought."

"Where did you find it?" Sarah asked.

"In the field, on the allotment. Someone has been burning things and this was in it. Where's Burgess?"

"Either at work or in the Inn, he hasn't come in yet."

"Are you sure?"

"He left here this morning and I haven't seen him since."

"You'd better go and check his room."

"What for?"

"See if his things are still there."

Sarah and Mary left the kitchen and went upstairs.

In the bedroom, Cockram was lying on the bed, after a hard day's work. The knock on the door aroused him and called out, "Come in!"

The door opened and Sarah and Mary walked in. Mary looked over Sarah's shoulder at Cockram and smiled seductively.

"Have you seen Will Burgess?" Sarah asked.

"No. I haven't seen him all day. Even at work," Cockram replied.

Mary moved to Sarah's side, Cockram saw her, sat up and smiled, as Sarah said, "Where's his belongings?"

Cockram looked away from Mary, when he realised Sarah was talking to him.

"Wha..." He got up and stood by the bed. "Eh, in the corner." He looked in the corner and pointed to a locked box. "There they are. Why?"

"Oh. Nothing," Sarah said.

Turning back to the women, Cockram asked, "What do you want with him?"

"We found..." Mary began to say, but was stopped when Sarah interrupted her saying, "Nothing. Sorry to disturb you."

Sarah turned and walked out of the room. Mary looked at Cockram with a coy smile on her face and when she realised that Sarah had left the room, she gave Cockram a wave goodbye, left the room and shut the door behind her.

Cockram had a big smile on his face when he jumped back on the bed and whispered Mary's name over and over again.

At the bottom of the stairs, when Mary caught up with Sarah, she looked at her and asked, "What are you going to do?"

"About him leaving? Nothing. But about this piece of pinafore, I'm taking it to Constable Taylor."

"But his belongings... Why did he leave the belongings, if he's gone?" Mary asked.

Sarah thought for a moment. "Because if he took them, then I would know he's left without paying the rent and left them there to say he's coming back. Besides, we're not sure he's coming back tonight; he's probably at a pub getting drunk. But why burn Anna's clothes if she's only gone to Porlock, he could get her back anytime. No, something's wrong and I better get the police involved."

"Do you think he's brought harm to her?"

"I don't know," Sarah replied, looking solemnly at Mary.

Chapter Seven

That evening in Simonsbath village, the Reverend William Thornton was riding his horse, Cochin China, through the village, when he came upon two men in conversation, twenty-nine-year-old, William court, who was the postmaster and thirty-nine-year-old, William Vellecott, who was Thornton's clerk. The men looked at Thornton and ran towards him.

Thornton leaned forward in the saddle, smiling at the two men, and asked, "What are you two yarning about?"

"Sir," answered Vellacott, "Little Anna Burgess. Her've disappeared. They can't find her anywhere. They'm all a-saying her father 'av done 'er in."

Thornton dismounted and looked sternly at the two men. "This is no light matter to make such an allegation."

"Sir, There 'av been rumours," Court said.

"Rumours, what rumours?" Thornton questioned.

"We were at the Gallon House an' we o'er heard a conversation."

"Go on."

"Burgess left the cot at six am He told Mrs. Marley the previous week, that 'e was taking his child to lodge in Porlock, at his sister's. He had taken a bundle containing the child's spare clothes, he 'ad returned alone that same evening."

"And, that does not mean he has killed her."

"A man had remarked to Sarah Marley, that somebody had been burning clothes in the Newtake at the back of the Gallon house. Mrs. Marley and two men went to 'ave a look and found ashes. She found a piece of scorched calico that looked like it had belonged to Anna Burgess's spare frock."

"And where's Burgess?" Thornton asked.

"He's disappeared."

"Now look here, Will Court. You shall pay for your suspicions. Go up to my house, take my chestnut mare and ride down immediately to Porlock, and when you get there, do not make a fool of yourself. Just look in and tell me that you have found the child alive and well. If by any chance the child is not there, say nothing about her, but enquire for William Burgess, and return to me."

William Court nodded and ran off. Thornton looked at Vellecott and said to him, "You. Don't say a word about anything. Understand?"

"Yes, sir," Vellacott replied.

"Because if he hasn't done anything to her, then we are trying to hang an innocent man. Now off with you."

Vellacott walked away and Thornton climbed back onto his horse. He sat there for a moment. As he watched Vellecott walk off, he shook his head and whispered, "I know he's a rogue and a thief, but I cannot believe he has killed that beautiful child," then gently kicking his horse with his heels, he commanded, "China, move on."

By the time Thornton arrived home and put China back into the stable, Court had just left. While the Reverend was taking the saddle off and was walking back into the vicarage, William Court was riding frantically across the moors to Porlock to gain the information the Reverend needed. Once Thornton settled down in his chair by the fire, he waited patiently for Court's return.

A few hours later, Thornton was still sitting in his chair. The room was plunged in darkness. The only light in the room was from the roaring fire. The lantern, on the small table next to him, was still unlit. As if transfixed by the bouncing flames, Thornton only shifted his gaze to the door when he heard a knock. He was about to get up, when he realised his wife had ran to answer the persistent knocking. She opened the door and William Court said, "Can I see the Reverend please? I have urgent news."

"Yes, of course, come in," Grace replied, closing the door on the excited Will Court.

"Thank you!"

As he entered the living room, Thornton stood up and lit the lantern on the table.

"Well," Thornton asked, "what news do you have?"

"He was at his sister's house that morning, alone," Court exclaimed, "Mr. Moore thought it strange, as he very rarely goes there."

"But the little girl wasn't with him?"

"No, sir."

"Right. Come with me."

"Where?"

"To Constable Fry's," Thornton said as he put his cloak on.

They both left the cottage under the bewildered gaze of the Reverend's wife.

At constable's house, forty-five-year-old William Fry, who was not only the village constable, but Sir Frederick Knight's nurseryman, opened the door and when he saw the two men standing there, he exclaimed, "Reverend Thornton, William! Come in," quite surprised at this unexpected visit.

After shutting the door, the three men walked back into the living room, where Fry said, "I was just about to retire for the night," as he turned to face the men.

Thornton said, "There will be plenty of time to sleep when we've caught a killer."

Looking shocked at the Reverend's remark, Fry replied, "A killer? Who?"

With a cold-steel look in his eyes, Thornton replied, "William Burgess."

"You mean, those burnt pieces of cloth, Mary Farley told me about, are little Anna Burgess's?"

"You knew about it?"

"Yes. Sarah Marley recognised the cloth."

"And what have you done about it?"

"Nothing. What is there to do? Just because some cloth was burnt, doesn't mean he's killed her. Besides, he told Sarah Marley, she's stopping with his sister's in Porlock."

"Have you been there to confirm this?"

Shaking his head, Fry replied, "No."

"Well it's a good job I sent Court there to find out."

"And I take it she is not there?"

"Correct."

Sitting down, Fry added, "Well, that's another matter then."

"Yes it is! So, in the morning, I want you to go to Lynmouth and find out if he's been there."

"Why Lynmouth?"

"Just a feeling I have. Will Court, here, will organise a search party and search the moors."

"And what will you do, sir?"

"Apart from praying for her, I will go to Taunton and consult with the Chief Constable."

"Chief Constable Goold? Right, I'll get on it first thing," Fry agreed, getting up, a visible sense of urgency in his eyes.

With everything planned, Thornton and Court left.

In the early hours of the morning, Thornton entered the stable. He looked at his horse and said, "Come on, boy. Work to be done."

He opened the stall and placed a blanket on the horse. He picked up the saddle, placed it on its back and tightened up the straps. He then placed the reins and bit over the horse's head and walked his mount out of the stable. When he shut the stable doors, he climbed into the saddle and as he patted the horse's mane, he said, "We've got a long way to go, boy. Move on." Thornton kicked his heels and China started off at a gallop.

The ride from Simonsbath to Taunton, took Thornton five hours. (It should be noted here, that in Reverend Thornton's memoirs, accounts differ from the reports in the *North Devon Journal*. Thornton wrote his memoirs forty years after the event, and I assumed that he went to Taunton to see the Chief Constable who would have told Thornton to get Superintendent Jeffs.)

When Thornton arrived, Chief Constable Goold sent him to Curry Rival, where Superintendent Jeffs lived. When he reached Jeffs's house, he got off his weary horse, rushed to the door and banged on it as hard as he could. An upstairs window opened and forty-two-year-old Cresant Jeffs appeared. He was in the middle of shaving. "Who's banging on my door at this time of the morning?" he shouted.

Looking up, Thornton answered, "Superintendent Jeffs?"

"Yes."

"I'm Reverend Thornton from Simonsbath."

"Simonsbath? What are you doing here then?" Jeffs asked.

"We have an incident involving a missing, possibly murdered child and an absconded father, who told everyone his daughter, was with his sister in Porlock, where she isn't."

Jeffs thought for a minute, and then shouted down, "I'll be right down and when I've had some breakfast, we'll go."

Thornton looked at his horse and then back up at Jeffs. "Give me some time. I've been riding since three o'clock this morning and my mare needs feeding."

"You must be hungry as well."

"I am."

"Take your mare and get it fed and come back for some breakfast."

"Thank you kindly."

Jeffs withdrew; shut the window and Thornton walked his horse to the stable.

Chapter Eight

Back on the moors, Court had organised a search party to explore the moorlands, in search of Anna's body, alive or dead. In the area behind the Gallon House Inn, a group of men were searching the fields. Two men were walking along a long trench of yellow earth that had been thrown up by mineral prospectors looking for veins, known as 'deads'. Both men in their forties, probing at the mud with a stick and when they found nothing, moved on. As they moved along the trench, one of the men poked his stick in the mud with signs of disturbance. He stopped, and looked back at his friend and said, "Look at this."

The second man walked up to him, looked down at the mud and knelt down.

The first man moved the top layer of the mud, the second man said, "Something's been laid here recently."

The second man dug in.

"Whatever was buried here isn't here no more."

The first man asked, "Do you reckon someone buried a stolen sheep there and came back when the coast was clear?"

"Could be. But it could have been something else."

"You'd better mark it," said the first man, "and we'll let Reverend Thornton know when he gets back."

The second man stuck his stick into the mud, got up and both men carried on searching.

At the same time at Lynmouth harbour, Constable Fry got off his pony-and-trap, tied it to a rail and walked along the harbour. He walked up to two fishermen, one in his forties and the other in his fifties, standing on their boat. Fry stood erect in front of them and said, "I'm looking for William Burgess. In his forties, dark hair, whiskers."

The first fisherman, who was the younger, replied, "Never seen him."

Fry looked at the older one and asked, "You?"

The older fisherman looked up at Fry, thought for a moment and replied, "Come to think of it, maybe I have. Better go and talk to Old Ned, over there."

The fisherman pointed and Fry looked over to another fishing boat with a man in his sixties, sorting out nets. Fry thanked the fishermen and walked over to old Ned and as he reached the boat, asked, "Old Ned?"

"Who be asking for him?" Old Ned replied, without looking up.

"Police."

Looking up, Old Ned said, "Police? I've done nothing wrong."

"Didn't say you have," Fry answered, "I'm looking for a man called William Burgess. In his forties, dark hair, whiskers."

Old Ned looked away and carried on sorting the nets. "Can't place him."

Turning back to the other fisherman, Fry said to Ned, "Your friends over there reckon you can."

Old Ned looked up and over at the other fishermen, "They do, do they? No don't know him."

Fry put his hand in his pocket, withdrew it and flicked a coin to Old Ned. Ned caught it, and said, "Ah, yes. I remember now. In a bit of a hurry. Wanted a ride on my boat."

"Where'd you take him?"

Old Ned pointed out to sea. "Across the water to Swansea."

Fry looked out to sea and looked at the outline of Wales across the Channel. "Did he say anything when going over?"

"Didn't take much notice. But if you ask me, I reckon he'd be looking for work at the new docks they're building over there."

"Did he say he was?"

"No. But there's money to be made o'er there for a man who wants it."

Fry thanked the old man, turned around and walked away. Old Ned flicked the coin up and caught it and looked over at the other fishermen, who looked back. Old Ned saw them looking and flicked the coin up again and smiled.

Thornton and Jeffs had been riding steadily side by side for a while when Jeffs asked, "What do you know of this Burgess, Reverend?"

"I've only known him just under two years and after our first meeting I marked him as a rogue."

"Why?"

"I had not long moved here from Lynmouth and he came to me, one day, with a heart-breaking story. He came to me and asked me if I could write him up a brief, as he was short of money as he had lost a pig and a valuable horse and he was struggling to keep his family fed and a roof over their heads."

Jeffs laughed. "That old trick, and did you?"

"I gave him a sovereign, but I refused to write him a brief, but a friend of mine, who was staying with me at the time, did."

"Well, that's not so bad. It only cost you a sovereign."

"Yes, but the brief that my friend wrote, Burgess got someone to put my name on it and stated that I gave him a sovereign. Then he took it around the villages."

"And obviously obtained some more money from them."

"Yes. Then one of Mr. Knights tenants, Mr. Bogie, an ex attorney, came to me, mad as hell. I asked him what was wrong. He said Burgess was a rogue and that he had deceived me with the story of the pig and pony and accused me of assisting Burgess to obtain money under false pretences."

"Didn't you report him to the local constable?"

"No. By the time Bogie told me, Burgess had raised enough money to last him a week, drinking in South Molton."

"So, what did you do?"

"Like I said, I just marked him as a rogue. I avoided Bogie for a while and after telling the parishioners about what Burgess had done, he avoided me."

"Do you think he killed the girl?"

Thornton thought for a minute, then replied, "A rogue and a sheep stealer, yes, but I find it hard to believe he killed his little girl."

"Well, when we find him, we'll find out where the girl is."

"If we find him."

"We'll find him and we'll find her."

Outside the Gallon House Inn, a group of people stood chatting amongst themselves. A man tapped another man and pointed over his shoulder. The second man looked around and saw Thornton and Jeffs riding towards them. The man ran up to Thornton and said, "Reverend! We've found a grave."

"Where?" Thornton asked.

"On the moor, behind the inn," the man said.

"Show us," Thornton demanded.

Without giving the Reverend an answer, the man started running. Thornton and Jeffs turned their horses and followed. The rest of the crowd didn't wait to being asked, they ran behind the three men.

They made their way to the trench where Thornton and Jeffs dismounted quickly and walked up to the empty grave.

Jeffs looked over Thornton's shoulder. Thornton looked closely at the line of yellowy brown earth and said, "It's just a line of deads."

"A what?" Jeffs' asked.

"The miners call them 'deads'," Thornton replied. "They dig a trench to discover the direction of mineral veins."

"So, it's nothing?"

"That is," one of the men said, "but this isn't," pointing to a disturbed part of earth.

Jeffs knelt down and looked at it.

"This looks like a little grave," Jeffs said.

"Probably someone buried some stolen sheep there," Thornton remarked.

Jeffs shook his head and replied, "Not this one."

"How can you tell?"

"Graves to deep and there's no sheep's hair in there."

"Well whatever was in there, has been taken out."

Jeffs stood up and looked at the second man and asked, "Have you checked the whole line?"

"Yes, sir."

Jeffs looked at the men and said, "Good work," then said to Thornton, "Let's go."

"Where?"

"Anywhere. There's nothing here."

As they were about to climb into the saddle, George Taylor, the thirty-three-year-old police Constable of Exford, rode up, jumped off his horse and said to Jeffs, "Sir, I heard you were here."

Jeffs looked at him. "What can I do for you, Constable?"

"Sir! I'd like to show you something. It's not far from here."

"What is it?"

"We found a spot where the little girl's clothes were burnt."

Intrigued, Jeffs said, "Show me."

When they got to the spot, they all dismounted and Taylor rummaged through the ashes, he looked up at Jeffs and Thornton, holding a handful of ashes, "Hooks and eyes from a girl's apparel."

"Obviously you've checked it's the Burgess girl's," Jeffs said.

"Yes, sir. Verified by Sarah Marley and Mary Farley," Taylor replied.

"Right! We'd better find this Burgess and find out where the girl is," Jeffs suggested, addressing Thornton. He looked back to Taylor and added, "Good work, Constable!"

Jeffs then returned his gaze to Thornton and nodded towards their mounts. The two men climbed into the saddle again.

"What now, sir?" Taylor asked.

"Now we find the bastard," Jeffs replied.

"I have Constable Fry checking Lynmouth," Thornton said, "Hopefully when we get back to the village, we should have some news."

"Lynmouth? Why Lynmouth?" Jeffs asked.

"Just a hunch I had."

"Lead on."

Jeffs and Thornton turned their horses and rode off.

When they reached Fry's cottage, Thornton and Jeffs climbed off their horses and knocked on the door. Constable Fry opened it, saw Jeffs and stood to attention. He saluted and said, "Hello, sir."

"Good Afternoon, Constable," Jeffs replied, returning the salute.

"Did you find anything?" Thornton asked.

"Yes, sir. Burgess has..."

"Not here," Jeffs interrupted, "...inside."

"Of course. Please come in."

Fry stood to one side to let the visitors in, and shut the door.

"We don't want to start a panic," Jeffs said to Fry.

"No, sir. Sorry, sir."

"What did you find out?" Thornton asked again.

"Burgess went to Lynmouth and on Friday," Fry replied, "crossed over to Swansea on Old Ned Groves's boat."

"Right," Jeffs said to Fry, "You and me are going to Swansea."

"When? How?" Fry asked.

"Now, and the same way Burgess got there, by boat."

Fry looked worried and nervously started to say something, but stopped himself.

"Do you have a problem with that, Constable?"

"N...No problem, sir."

As they left Fry's cottage, Thornton collected his horse and went back to the vicarage.

Leaving his horse tied to a post outside the cottage, Jeffs climbed up on Fry's pony-and-trap and made their way to Lynmouth.

When they got to Lynmouth, Jeffs commandeered Old Ned's boat and the old man took the officers over to Wales. Halfway across, Jeffs was standing on the bow of the boat as Fry staggered over to him, looking ill; Fry didn't like sailing and he knew he wasn't going to like the journey.

Jeffs looked at him and asked, "Are you alright?"

"Yes, sir. I just don't like travelling on boats."

"Why didn't you say so, man? I would have brought someone else."

"I didn't like to say and I want to get Burgess as much as any man."

"Well, when we do get him, I hope you're alright to travel back."

"I will, sir. Sir? What if he's not at the new docks, how are we going to find him?"

"Oh, he'll be there."

"But what if he isn't?"

Jeffs looked sharply at Fry. "Then we'll have to extend the search, won't we?"

As Fry sat down, head over the side, ready to be sick, Jeffs looked across the water to the coast of Wales.

C. R. Woollands

Chapter Nine

By the time they landed in Wales, and searched all the places that were under construction, Jeffs and Fry ran out of time to find Burgess. They took a room for the night. The next day, on the 19th of August, they continued their search, which again took most of the day, until they walked up to a works' supervisor and enquired about Burgess, who nodded and pointed him out for Jeffs. Cautiously Jeffs and Fry walked up behind Burgess as not to spook him and run off, but to Jeffs surprise, Burgess never ran.

"William Burgess?" Jeffs called.

Burgess turned around sharply, looked at the men and replied, "Yes."

"William Burgess. I am Superintendent Jeffs. I am here..."

"I done it and I must die for it. I would sooner die than live, for I shall never be happy any more. But I would have saved you the trouble of fetching me by making away with myself and I ought to have done it before."

Jeffs nodded at Fry, who walked behind Burgess and put handcuffs on him.

Looking at his watch, he said to Fry, "We'll have to stay in Swansea tonight and make our way back tomorrow when the tide is right."

"Where will we stay?" Fry asked.

"We put him at the local station. Then, we'll have to try that lodging house we stayed in last night."

Fry nodded and pulled Burgess, but Burgess resisted and said, "There's my box that is at Marley's. I should like it given to my second daughter, and the money I have in my pocket and my clothes to my boy, for they'll be no more use to me."

"We'll sort that out later. Let's go," Jeffs replied.

"My belongings that are at my lodgings...," Burgess shouted.

"Let's get you tucked away behind bars first and then we'll get your belongings to take back with us," Jeffs said.

Jeffs and Fry walked Burgess off.

While Jeffs and Fry were in Swansea, Thornton continued the search for Anna's body. Thornton had no difficulty in finding volunteers, and gangs of men were soon poking, peeping, enquiring all over Exmoor. By Thursday night, as Thornton climbed wearily into bed, there was no sign of Anna's body anywhere. At Midnight, he was awoken by a shower of stones flung against the window. He sat up as another stone hit the window. Thornton got out of bed and as he walked to the window he shouted, "What now?"

Thornton opened the window and looked down at a young villager, by the name of William Kingdom. Kingdom was in his early twenties and was a blacksmith, like his father before him, also called William.

"What is it?" Thornton shouted down.

"They've got him," Kingdom replied.

"Burgess? I'll be right down."

Thornton shut the window, slipped into his trousers, threw a dressing gown over his shoulder and left the room.

As most villages around that area at the time, news travelled faster than a locomotive and before the horse and trap had reached the village, villagers had gathered, some in their nightshirts and bed gowns, outside Fry's house, waiting to see the suspected murderer, William Burgess.

Thornton moved through the crowd as the pony-and-trap pulled up. Jeffs and Fry got down and pulled Burgess off the back. The crowd part as Jeffs and Fry escorted Burgess to the house. As they got to the door, Thornton stopped them and looked at Burgess.

"Burgess!" Thornton said, "If ever you were in need of a friend, it is now. I'm your clergyman and I'll do what I can, but you must tell me what you've done with Anna."

Burgess looked shocked at Thornton's outburst, but did not answer and looked away. As he did so, Thornton shouted at him, "Murderer!" He then turned to the crowd and said, "Look at him. His silence convicts him. Here he stands; the very worst kind of murderer."

Fry, fearing the crowd would attack Burgess, took the prisoner inside his cottage and stayed with him.

Jeffs pulled Thornton to one side and said, "What you've done is to hamper the case by letting him know we haven't found the body. Now he'll never speak."

Thornton looked at Jeffs and calmly replied, "We'll find the body yet. I'll promise you that."

"They'd better, because without a body we'll have to let him go."

He ran his eyes over the crowd and said to Thornton, "Is the Marley woman here?"

Thornton looked around and when he spotted Sarah Marley, he called out, "Sarah Marley! Can you come here, please?"

Sarah Marley walked through the crowd to Jeffs and Thornton.

Jeffs said to her, "Mrs. Marley, can you come in please?"

Sarah looked worried at Thornton, who replied, "It's okay. I'll come with you."

Inside the cottage, Superintendent Jeffs asked her, "Mrs. Marley. I would like to show you something and I'm hoping you can recognise them."

Jeffs then took a small pair of boots out of a bag and showed them to her.

"They're Anna's," Mrs. Marley replied. "She was wearing them the morning she left my house." She began to cry. "Oh, the poor girl. What could he have done with her?"

"When we find the body, we'll find out. We're taking him to Dulverton shortly and hopefully by then we'd have found her," Jeffs said.

On Friday, the 20th of August, in the morning before daylight, Jeffs and Fry walked out of the cottage with Burgess, put him in the cart, covered him with a blanket and proceeded out of the village toward Dulverton.

On the next day, Saturday 21st in his gaol cell in Dulverton, Constable Taylor, who knew the prisoner well, took him some breakfast and a cup of coffee. Burgess at this time was aware that the game was up. When Taylor opened the door and entered, carrying a tray with the breakfast and cup of coffee on it, Burgess sat up on the cot. He was handcuffed. Taylor placed the tray on a table and uncuffed the prisoner, so he could eat his breakfast.

Taylor had turned his back on Burgess for a brief moment, when Burgess jumped up, pushed Taylor to the floor and picked up a pair of scissors from the table. Burgess held the scissors in his hand menacingly, and then plunged the scissors into his own throat.

"My God," Taylor yelled, and then shouted, "Quick, help me in here!"

Taylor struggled with Burgess for a moment, before Sergeant Edmunds, another officer from Dulverton entered the cell to help Taylor overpower Burgess and pulled the scissors from his throat. Blood squirted out but Taylor contained the bleeding.

"Get a doctor," shouted Edmunds as Taylor ran out of the cell.

Burgess looked up at Edmunds and said with a slur as blood came from his mouth, "It's all right; I'm going to die now."

Keeping Burgess restrained, Edmunds replied, "You'll die, but not here. You're not going to deprive the hangman from his job."

Doctor John Barrett-Collyns appeared on the scene a short while later. He attended and treated Burgess's injury. After the doctor had stitched the wound, Jeffs asked him, "Is he going to be alright?"

"Yes. I've stopped the bleeding and as long as he doesn't touch the stitches, he'll live. He was lucky he didn't stab anything vital; he was millimetres from the jugular vein. If he hit that he would be dead."

Jeffs looked at the officers and asked, "How did this happen?"

Taylor answered, "I took off his handcuffs for a cup of coffee; he jumped up, pushed me to the floor and picked up a pair of scissors from the table. I thought he was going to attack me with them, but he stabbed himself."

"Why was a pair of scissors in here in the first place?" Jeffs asked.

Taylor shook his head and replied, "I do not know, sir."

Jeffs looked down at Burgess, who looked back at him.

Groaning now, the prisoner said, "It's all right, I'm going to die now and that's all I care about, for I don't want to be dragged about the country."

"Well, I don't know about being dragged about the country, but you're being taken before the magistrate this morning." Jeffs turned to Taylor and said, "Keep an eye on him. I don't want anymore incidents."

"Yes, sir," Taylor said.

That same morning, Burgess was brought up before the magistrate of the Dulverton bench, forty-two-year-old John A. Locke, Esq., and fifty-four-year-old, Capt. William Bernard. When evidence of a formal nature had been deposed, the prisoner was remanded for a week. Burgess was brought to Taunton in a trap, and left in the custody of Superintendent Jeffs and Sergeant Edmunds. The same evening, William Burgess was incarcerated in the county gaol.

The Wheal Eliza Murder

Chapter Ten

Sunday service at St. Luke's Church in Simonsbath, on the 22nd of August, was unlike any other services in parishes or towns in the land.

Reverend Thornton stood at the pulpit. He looked out at his parishioners and preached, "And Cain talked with Abel his brother; and it came to pass, when they were in the field, that Cain rose up against Abel and slew him. The despicable crime of murder, unique as destroying someone made in God's image, and acient going back to Cain killing Abel. Abel's blood cried out for vengeance and so will this blood. The omniscience of God sees and knows everything and will bring secret things to light in the day of judgement. There is mercy for the chief of sinners. Let this man come forward and acknowledge his crime and cast himself on the mercy of God. He must pay the supreme penalty because Genesis 9:6 demands that those who shed man's blood by man shall their blood be shed for they have killed one made in the image of God. But they will escape the flames of Hell in the life to come if they bring commensurate repentance to God. So one would end with exhortations to pray for this man."

When the service ended, Thornton stood at the door of the church as the parishioners left. As he said goodbye to them, a woman from the village stopped and said to him, "I hope they find that poor child soon, Reverend."

"They will. With God's help, we'll find her," Thornton replied.

As the woman scurried off, Jeffs walked up to him while the rest of the parishioners were leaving.

Thornton said to Jeffs, "Any news?"

"No," Jeffs replied. "We've taken him to Taunton gaol and we've got a further remand until next Saturday."

"We'll find her."

"I hope so," Jeffs said, leaving the Reverend on the Church's front steps.

On Wednesday, the 25th of August, Constable Fry was going around the village, putting up handbill's that were printed up the day before. On the board outside his house, villagers were reading the handbill, it read:

£10 REWARD

Whereas I have received information which leads me to suppose that a girl, of six years of age, named Anna Burgess, has been murdered and her body concealed either on Exmoor Forest or in the vicinity of Porlock; I am therefore authorised to offer a Reward of Ten Pounds to any Person who shall discover the said Body. Should the body be found, the person finding it, is requested not to move it, or remove anything on it; but immediately to communicate the circumstances to the nearest Police Constable, or to Mr. Superintendent Jeffs, at Exford. The above Reward will be paid by Valentine Goold, Esquire, Chief Constable, to any person who may become entitled to it under the conditions of this notice.

CRESANT JEFFS, Superintendent.
Dated, Exford, August 24th 1858.

Going home, after leaving the inn, the two men that were a week before, planning on taking a sheep's carcass from a dead on the moors with Burgess, were walking towards the village. One looked up towards the sky over the Birchcleave woods. He saw a strange blueish light in the sky and only in one place. He pointed up and said to his friend, "Look at that."

His friend looked up and replied, "My God. I've never seen anything like that before. Is it the moonlight?

"No," said the first man, "and even if it was, it wouldn't give that bluey light."

"It's weird," said the other man as they walked on, still looking at the strange light. But as they continued to walk, the first man looked puzzled and then as the men parted company, the first man, ran as fast as he could to Simonsbath.

Fast asleep in their bed Mrs. Thornton was woken up by stones tapping against the window. She nudged her husband, who, with all the rushing around he had done, was dead to the world. But after a couple more nudges, he woke up.

"William! William!" she said. "Someone's throwing something at the window."

Thornton got out of bed and turned up the lantern. Another stone was thrown at the window, as Thornton walked over to the window and looked out, all he could see was the ground and bushes in the darkness. He opened the window and leaned out.

"Who's there?" he shouted down.

From the darkness a voice called out, "Rev. Thornton?"

"Yes. Who is it?"

Still not showing himself, the man replied, "Sir, if I tell you something, that might be worth hearing, will 'ee keep it quiet about me?"

"Yes."

"Well, me and my friend were up to no good..."

"This isn't the time and place to confess any sins..." Thornton shouted down. And as he was about to close the window, the man's words stopped him. "I'm not! But it's why I want to keep my identity a secret."

Intrigued, Thornton leaned back out and said, "Go on."

"Well, me and my friend came across, what looked like a grave among the deads and we thought someone had buried a dead sheep there and we thought we would go back later to collect it and make some money."

"And?"

"We met up with someone else to help us and arranged to go back after dark."

"If you are keeping you and your friend's identity a secret am I to assume that you are keeping your other friends name a secret?"

"No, sir."

"Then can you tell me who the third man was?"

The voice hesitated for a moment then called out, "William Burgess!"

"Burgess?"

"Yes. It was on a Tuesday night in July. We were in the Gallon House and we planned to meet up with Burgess after dark."

"Go on."

"Well, Burgess never showed up and me and my friend didn't go through with it."

"Good man!"

"Not so good, since I went for a walk on the moor. Don't ask what for, sir, and I won't lie to you. But I was walking on the hillside above the Wheal Eliza mine, and I heard footsteps from below me going in that direction."

From his window, Thornton could see the outline of the mine site in the far distance. He fixed his gaze upon the shadows and he too saw the bluish, hazy light in the sky. Trembling from head to toe, he whispered, "Of course, why didn't I think of that? The mine. She's showing us where she is." He looked back down to the man in the darkness. "Okay, thank you for the information and although I know who you are, your identity will be safe with me."

Thornton shut the window with shaking hands, walked to a chair by the bed, and said gleefully, "At last, we've got him."

Wearily, half asleep, Grace Thornton asked, "Got who?"

"Burgess. I think... No, I'm sure I know where Anna's body is," Thornton replied as he started to get dressed.

Sitting up, Grace looked at her husband astonished. "What are you doing?"

"I've got to go to Dulverton."

"What? Now?"

"No sooner the time to tighten the rope around his neck."

"Okay," she replied, "But I don't think whoever you plan to see, will thank you for getting them out of bed in the middle of the night. Why don't you leave it until the morning?"

Looking at the clock and realising what time it was, Thornton said, "Yes, dear, I think you're right."

He took off his trousers and climbed back into bed.

The next morning after riding to Dulverton, Thornton stood in the office where the Magistrate, John Locke, a portly forty-two-year-old man, was sitting.

"I've had information given to me by an anonymous source that Anna Burgess's body is at the Wheal Eliza Mine," Thornton said.

"Where about's at the mine?" the magistrate asked.

"From the information I was told, I would presume down the mineshaft."

"And your reason to presume the mineshaft?"

"Burgess didn't have time to dig another grave and throwing the body down the shaft would have been quicker."

"Very well, Reverend. We'll arrange the shaft emptied of water and get someone to search it. If nothing is found, then we'll pay the bill ourselves."

"Thank you, but I have a hunch, we will find her there."

The magistrate knew that they would find something and said to Thornton, "I'll put some tenders out and once we get someone to do it, we'll commence."

On Saturday morning Burgess was taken from the county gaol in Taunton, to Dulverton, for re-examination before the magistrates. He was wearing a sparkled velveteen shooting jacket with metallic buttons of sporting pattern, brown cloth vest, coloured cotton neckerchief, corduroy breaches, and drab gaiters.

On his arrival at Dulverton, a large crowd of spectators thronged the approaches to the market house, over which the petty session's room was situated; and near the entrance to the Red Lion Hotel, where two officers climbed down from the pony-and-trap and helped Burgess down. As they made their way to the hall, many in the crowd that had assembled, jeered at Burgess, shouting,

"Murderer! Murderer!" Amid the throng, Burgess's daughter, Mary, was watching. She was dressed in black, and had walked that morning from Withypool to see her father tried.

While in the passage of the inn, Burgess pointed out his daughter to one of the police constables, "That's my daughter, Mary."

Taylor looked at her and asked Burgess, "Do you want to talk to her?"

Burgess looked at his daughter and said to Taylor, "I have nothing to say to her."

As Burgess was taken through, he turned to his daughter and shouted, "What do you do here? You have no business here at all."

Mary didn't answer and just watched as the officers took Burgess before the magistrates. Immediately before the court was opened for admission to the public, Burgess noticing his daughter, Mary, in the room he said to her again, "You have no business here at all."

The Magistrates, John A. Locke Esq., and Captain William Bernard, took the bench. Mr. Valentine Goold, the chief constable, attended to watch the case on the part of the prosecution. The depositions of the various witnesses were taken down by Mr. Samuel Warren, solicitor, who had been recently appointed Clerk to the Justices. Captain Bernard, hit the bench with his gavel and when the crowd had quietened down, he said, "Mr. Warren, call your first witness."

Mr. Warren stood up and shouted, "I call William Cockram."

Cockram stood up and walked to the box and after swearing in, said, "I am William Cockram; I live at Exford, in the County of Somerset, and am a labourer. I lodged with the prisoner during the month of July last, at a cottage, situated near the Gallon House, in the parish of Exford. I slept in the same bed with the prisoner; on Sunday, the 25th July, the prisoner turned out of his bed at half-past three o'clock in the morning. He said, "William, will you please to tell me what time it is?" He unhung my watch which was hanging by the side of the bed, and handed it to me; I looked at the watch and saw it was half-past-three. The prisoner dressed himself and went downstairs; he did not say where he was going. The prisoner's daughter Anna aged six years, slept in the same bed with us; after he had dressed himself, he said to his daughter, "Anna, come, turn out," the child got up, and left the room with him. I saw the prisoner again on the evening of the same day, between nine and ten o'clock, in our lodgings; he was in the bed that I sleep in. I have not seen the child since; she did not return with him.

Mr. Warren looked at Burgess and asked, "Burgess, do you wish to ask this man any questions?"

Burgess stood up and looked at Warren and replied, "Well, sir, I baint going to ask him nothing."

Warren looked at Goold and said, "Any more questions?" Goold shook his head and Warren said to Cockram, "Thank you. You may step down now." When Cockram had seated himself, Warren said, "I call Mrs. Sarah Marley."

Sarah Marley stood up and walked to the box and when she was sworn in, said, "My name is Sarah Marley, I am the wife of John Marley, of Exford, labourer.

The prisoner, William Burgess, lodged with me at Gallon House Cottages, in that parish. About two months since the prisoner came to lodge at my house, and continued as my lodger up to the 10th of August. The prisoner's daughter, Anna Maria, lived with me, and the prisoner paid me half a crown a week for her maintenance. The child was about six years old, and I believe was with me about three weeks. On Saturday, the 24th of July last, the prisoner told me to clean her and get her clothes ready, as he was going to take her to Porlock to his sister's. I cleaned the child and got her clothes ready; I put into a bundle one flannel petticoat, three cotton frocks, one of lilac colour, one brown or chocolate colour, and one a light colour with stripes in it, and a fur victorine; three were tied up in a cotton handkerchief. The prisoner left the pinafore, part of which is now produced, with me on the 19th of August. The child had two pinafores of the pattern now produced by P.C. George Taylor."

A man held up a piece of burnt cotton print of lilac colour and was shown to the witness.

"Is this the piece of cloth, Mrs. Marley?" Warren asked.

Sarah looked at it and replied, "Yes. That is of the same colour and pattern as the child's pinafore. The piece of fur produced is of the same description as the fur victorine I tied up in the child's bundle. The piece of burnt serge now also produced is the same description of material as the petticoat I put in the bundle; there was also tied up in the bundle of clothes two pairs of black yarn stockings of the same pattern as the piece produced. The child had one pair of boots and one pair of shoes; she went away in the boots, and I bought the only pair of shoes she had off the prisoner, on the morning of the 10th of August. I was in the habit of lacing up or tying her boots, as she could not do it herself; I did it every day. I have examined the boots now produce by Superintendent Jeffs and I believe they are the same boots she had on when she left. I have not seen the child since I saw her go into the prisoner's bedroom on Saturday 24th of July. The child did not return on the Sunday evening. A few days after the prisoner returned to my house, I asked him whether there were many children where the child was, and he replied, "Yes, but she is not going to stay there long."

The prisoner paid for its maintenance regularly; he once told me he thought half a crown was too much, but I told him I did not think it was. I told him I would keep her and use her as a child of my own, if he would leave her with me. The prisoner returned to my house about three o'clock on Sunday the 25th of July."

Mr. Warren looked at Burgess and asked, "Burgess, do you wish to ask her any question?"

Without standing up, Burgess looked at Sarah and said, "No; that's plenty for herself and me too."

Warren looked at Goold who again shook his head. Warren turned to Sarah, thanked her and told her to step down and called the next witness.

"My name is John Mills, I am a labourer, and work on the farm of my father, at the Gallon House, Exmoor, in this county. On Wednesday morning the 11th of August, as I was going to work, crossing one of my father's fields, I saw that there had been a fire on one of the allotments. I went up and examined it, but could not tell what had been burnt; it was a heap or mound in the form of a beehive; I put my foot upon it and broke it in. I then went on to my work. On the next day in the evening I was passing through the same allotment with my brother; when I came up to the spot, I called my brother's attention to it. I took a stick and moved the heap about and there I saw some buttons, and hooks and eyes and pieces of cotton print, also a piece of fur.

The article now produced by P.C. Taylor is the same as I found in the heap when I stirred it about."

Mary Farley was called next and she said to the court, "I am a single woman, and live at Gallon House cottage, in the parish of Exford. On Sunday the 15th of August, I went up to Mr. Mills' allotment to see where the fire had been, and I there picked up a piece of lilac cotton print, and a piece of a black yarn stocking. I know the bit of print as a piece of Anna Burgess's pinafore; I had seen it at Sarah Marley's, because I had washed there. I have washed the pinafore. I took the things I picked up to Sarah Marley's with whom the child had been living. I asked her if she knew it, and she said, "Yes, it is a piece of Anna Burgess's pinafore."

Mr. Goold stood up and asked her, "Had you any conversation with the prisoner at any time?"

"Yes, sir," she replied.

"Tell the magistrates," Mr. Goold asked.

Mary looked at the magistrates and said, "I saw the prisoner about six weeks ago, when he said, "I am going to leave the country," I said, "Where are you going to? Be you going to take the little maid with you?" the prisoner replied, "Yes, I be."

Burgess stood and angrily said, "Tell all thee knowest, and thee'st get a job; thee'it ne'er get another, perhaps."

Warren said to him, "What she says now is nothing that we take notice of. Do you ask her anything as to what she has said before?"

"No, sir; because they'll swear a white sheep's a black 'un, the whole lot of them – everybody knows that," Burgess replied.

Warren looked at Goold, who knowing if he had any questions, shook his head. He turned to Mary and thanked her and told her to step down and recalled Sarah Marley. When she took the stand again, Warren asked her if she could confirm what Mary Farley had said, and Sarah replied, "Yes sir. I recollect the 15th day of August.

On that day the last witness, Mary Farley, came to my house; she brought the piece of cotton lilac print and piece of stocking produced, and I kept them until I handed them over to George Taylor, the policeman."

Warren thanked Sarah Marley and called George Taylor.

"I am George Taylor; I am a police constable, stationed at Exford; on Monday the 16th of August, I went with Superintendent Jeffs, to the allotment belonging to Mr. Mills, where the fire had been. I picked up several hooks and eyes, some fragments of tinder, and other things; they have been in my possession ever since."

Superintendent Jeffs was called next and when he was sworn in said, "I am Mr. Cresant Jeffs; I am Superintendent, 2nd class of the Wiveliscombe division. On Thursday, the 19th of August, I apprehended the prisoner at Swansea. I took him to his lodgings for the purpose of getting possession of his things; I searched him, and in his bag where his clothes were I found these boots. On the 21st of August, I took the boots out of the prisoner's bag in his presence, and he said, "They are a pair of boots I bought for my boy." The boots are the same that have been identified by the witness Sarah Marley as having belonged to the child Anna Maria Burgess. This witness's deposition, taken on the prisoner's first examination, was then read as follows: -

"From information received on Wednesday last the 18th instant, I proceeded to Exmoor, in the county of Somerset, and in a field distant two fields from the back of the 'Red Deer Inn,' I found the spot where some female wearing apparel had been burned. I then went to a field where I was informed the prisoner had previously been at work; this field is about a mile distant from the field in which I found the remains of the clothes. There, I saw a hole, which had the appearance of a grave, it was between 3 and 4 feet long and 2 feet wide in the centre, and about 2 to 3 feet deep. From other information I received, I commenced a search for the prisoner; I traced him to Lynmouth, in the county of Devon, and from thence to Swansea. I found him at work at the new docks now in course of erection there. I took him aside from the other men, and told him I wished to speak to him about his youngest daughter. He turned very pale and appeared confused, and said, "It's all right." I then told him I should arrest him on suspicion of murdering his child. He said, "I done it and must die for it. I would sooner die than live; I shall never be happy no more." And then said, "My box that is at Exmoor I should like given to my second daughter at North Molton, the money that is in my pocket and my clothes, you give to my boy."

I then took him towards the police station at Swansea, and he repeated many times, "I would sooner die than live. I shall never be happy no more; I would have saved you the trouble to come and fetch me; I would have made away with myself; I ought to have done so before." He then asked, "Have my other children seen it?"

These remarks were quite voluntary on the part of the prisoner, and were not in consequence of my asking questions. I searched him and found two pounds, six shillings and a half penny in his pockets, also the key of his box."

The last witness of the day was called and William Fry stood in the witness box.

"I am William Fry, I am a labourer and local constable acting for and living in the parish of Exmoor. On the morning of the 18th of August, I accompanied the superintendent to Swansea; we went to the new docks, where we arrested the prisoner. After we had arrested him, the prisoner was handcuffed to me; and as we were going along towards the Quay, he said to me, "Have they found the maid?" I said, "Burgess, you may very well suppose that they have."

Mr. Warren and Mr. Goold had finished questioning the witness' and at that stage of the proceeding, Mr. Goold having consulted with the magistrates, said he would defer taking this witness's examination until the next sitting. Mr. Superintendent Jeffs then applied for a further remand until Saturday next, when he expected to be able to produce some important evidence.

The bench granted the application, and the accused was re-committed to Taunton Gaol.

The Wheal Eliza Murder

Chapter Eleven

After Thornton's request and the inquest at the weekend, Chief Constable Goold placed adverts in the local papers, looking for a diver for the purpose of examining every nook and cranny of the Wheal Eliza Mine. He also put the advert in *The Times* and the *Builder, Mining Journal*, and *Journal of Practical Engineering*.

The advert ran as follows:

To MINERS and DIVERS. – WANTED, by the Chief Constable of Somerset, a PERSON competent, and who has all the necessary apparatus, to descend into several copper mines shafts, full of water, for the purpose of seeking the body of a child, supposed to have been thrown down one of them. There are five shafts, two of which are at least 240 feet in depth. They are all situated in Exmoor Forest in the county of Somerset. Application, stating terms, etc. to be made to VALENTINE GOOLD, Esq, Glastonbury, county of Somerset.
Dated August 30, 1858.

On the 4th of September 1858, forty-year-old Henry Sully, chief warder of Taunton gaol and thirty-two-year-old, Sergeant Benjamin Judd of the county police, brought Burgess back to Dulverton for examination before the same magistrates, John Locke, and Captain Bernard. There were only a few people in the court room watching the procedure and as Burgess entered the room it was noticed that he looked paler than he was at his last examination and that his manner was less defiant and calmer. The only witness to be examined was Burgess's brother-in-law, John Moore, and Superintendent Jeffs asked him questions.

After swearing in he was asked what he knew about the prisoner and he answered, "I am John Moore of the parish of Porlock, Somerset. I am a labourer and I know the prisoner, William Burgess; as he is my brother-in-law."

"How well do you know the prisoner?" Jeffs asked.

"I have known him well for fourteen or fifteen years," Moore replied.

"Do you know how many children the prisoner has?"

"I do not know how many children he has."

"Have you seen his youngest child?"

"I never in my life saw his youngest."

"When was the last time you saw the prisoner?"

"I recollect his coming to my house on Sunday morning, the 25th July, between seven and eight o'clock."

"And he was on his own, no child with him?"

"He did not bring any child with him on that occasion."

"Are you sure?"

"He never brought a child to my house, nor had he talked to me about it previously, or anything of the sort."

"How long did he stay at your house that morning?" Jeffs asked.

"He had his breakfast and remained at my house about three quarters of an hour."

"What was his condition when he arrived at your house?"

"His clothes were very wet, and he had taken off his stockings and leggings to dry when I saw him."

"Why was that, Mr. Moore?"

"It had been raining much that morning," replied Moore, "I and my wife were in bed when the prisoner came and knocked at the back door; our little maid lighted a fire, and we then got up and dressed."

"Mr. Moore. The prisoner told people he was taking his daughter to a relative's in Porlock. Does the prisoner have any other relatives there about's?" Jeffs said.

"I do not know that the prisoner has any other relations living in Porlock, except his mother, who is bed-ridden, and lives with me."

"Please remind me what your relationship is to the prisoner?"

Moore looked strangely at Jeffs and replied, "I married his sister."

Jeffs turned to Burgess and said, "Do you have any questions for the witness?"

Burgess looked up at Moore and shook his head. Jeffs asked Moore to step down and addressed the bench, "There are no more witnesses and I ask the bench for a further remand of the prisoner for another week.

"Can I ask why another week?" Bernard asked.

Chief Constable Goold stood up and said, "We then shall be in a position, your worships, to submit the entire evidence to you."

The magistrates conferred with each other and Captain Bernard said to the court, "The prisoner will be remanded for another week and we will reconvene here next Saturday."

He hit the gavel on the bench and everybody stood up.

Burgess was put back in handcuffs and taken back to Taunton.

The following week was a busy one for the magistrates, the Chief Constable and Superintendent Jeffs, as tenders flooded in with offers to descend the now disused copper mines of Wheal Eliza. (Here, there is another discrepancy between newspapers and official records of the day. According to The Taunton Courier of Wednesday, the 16th of September 1858 the owner of the mine was a Captain Dunstan. However, Captain William Dunstan left the mine in June 1854. A Mr. W. Williams took over and because no workable copper could be found, the lease of the mine was assigned to Sir Frederick Knight for the sum of £328.17.6d through William Thomas Whyte on the 5th of June 1855. Knight searched the mines for iron, which also proved a disappointment. It was then leased to a company called Schneider and Hannay of Ulverton. The mine was dewatered and prospecting commenced, again disappointingly, and finally, early in the year of 1857, all operations ceased and the mines closed down.)

On the morning of the 11th of September, Burgess was brought up in the custody of Mr. Sully, chief warder of Taunton gaol, and acting-sergeant Williams, of the county police, at Dulverton, for examination.

Forty-one-year-old, magistrate Fenwick Bissett, joined John Locke and Captain Bernard on the bench, and even though there was only one witness to be examined, the justice room was densely crowded.

Mr. Warren examined William Smith, a shoemaker and publican, living at North Molton, who stated that he "had known the prisoner since the 30th of May last; about the time Burgess attended a club, which was held at his house. The 30th of May was on a Sunday, and the club meeting was held on the following day. The prisoner gave him an order for a pair of boots for his little girl, a child about six years old. A day or two after the club day, a woman named Jane Ford, with whom Burgess and his daughter lodged, brought a little girl to his house to be measured for the boots. He thought the child was about six years of age. He took her measurements, and the boots were made in his shop by his son, and when finished he sent them to Jane Ford's for the child. In a week or two after he had measured the child's feet, he saw the prisoner again, and he appeared angry that the boots were not made. The boots produced by Superintendent Jeffs' witness were identified as those made in his shop by the prisoner's order and sent to Ford's."

The evidence taken on the three former examinations was then read over, after which, Mr. Fenwick Bissett, the chairman, gave the usual caution, and asked the prisoner whether, after such caution, he wished to say anything?

"No," Burgess said sullenly.

Mr. Warren, the magistrate's clerk, having written down the prisoner's answer, asked him if he would sign it.

Burgess started throwing out his arms with violence and shouted, "No, I shall have nothing more to do wi' it. Do what you like with me; you can't do more nor you have; but I don't care, they've all swore false."

The magistrates then informed the prisoner that he stood fully committed for trial at the next assizes, for the wilful murder of his daughter, Anna Maria Burgess.

Mr. Superintendent Jeffs was bound over to prosecute and give evidence in the trial; and Burgess was handcuffed and ironed, taken back to the county gaol at Taunton.

Following the examination, the magistrates, Superintendent Jeffs and Chief Constable Goold met in another room to meet the successful tender for the mine, Mr. Morris Howard. Mr. Howard was a professional diver from the firm of Saddler and Company, Tooley Street, London, manufacturers of the patent diving and submarine apparatuses. He was taken, the same afternoon, with Superintendent Jeffs, to Exmoor, to prove the depths of the shafts there. On examining the Wheal Eliza shafts, Howard found that there was 100 feet of water or upwards to be pumped out before it would be possible for him or any diver to descend with the least chance of success. The following day, Mr. Howard returned to London, to await the result of an attempt to get a considerable body of water out of the mine.

The following week Mr. Warren drew up an advert for engineers to help empty the mine. The advert went like this:

COUNTY OF SOMERSET
TO ENGINEERS AND OTHERS

THE MAGISTRATES acting for the division of Dulverton, in the County of Somerset, are desirous of receiving tenders, FROM persons willing to undertake a CONTRACT FOR PUMPING THE WATER OUT OF A CERTAIN MINE SHAFT, situated on Exmoor in the above County. The shaft contains about 250 feet of water, and it is required, that the contractor should clear the shaft, so that only 60 feet of water be left therein. There is erected close to the shaft, a WATER-WHEEL, with Water Carriage, Pump, etc., complete, which, at a slight expense, may be made available for the purpose tenders for the above work to be addressed, before the 2nd of October next to Mr. Warren, the

specifications may be seen, and further particulars obtained.
Dulverton, September 18th 1858.

This advert went into the local papers and other concerned national papers throughout the week.

C. R. Woollands

Chapter Twelve

With Burgess committed to Taunton gaol until the winter assizes, the search for Anna's body by the authorities were by no means relaxed. In their endeavour to bring light to the murder of the unfortunate victim of this atrocious crime, and although their efforts had yet proved unavailing, no pains or expense was spared to carry out the search of every part of the mine.

On the 16th of October, twenty-nine-year-old mining engineer, Thomas Skewes from Molland in Devonshire and his partner John Moffat, who were given the contract for pumping out the mine, started work. Although the authorities knew the work would take some time, people from the village and afar, watched anxiously, Reverend Thornton among them.

The squelching sound of the water, slowly running out of the pump into the nearby river Barle and the sound of the water wheel, echoed throughout the valley.

With news of every amount of water emptied from the shaft travelling around the village, Thornton and Jeffs knew at that time, they were not needed at the mine. After being invited to stay at the vicarage, instead of travelling back to Taunton, Jeffs followed Thornton to his home. That evening they sat in front of a brightly burning fire before retiring to bed.

"He's not saying anything," Jeffs said as they both sipped a fine port, "…just sits in his cell, looking at the wall. You told me about him being a rogue and a sheep stealer; do you know anything else about his background?"

Putting his glass on the table next to his chair, Thornton replied, "Not a lot. When he pulled that trick with the brief, I asked around about him."

"What did you find out?"

"Nothing that I hadn't surmised. He comes from Porlock. Can't read, nor write, but can drink and get into fights. From what I've heard and seen, he doesn't have many friends and his other four children were put out to service."

"Are you sure?"

"Yes. After what has happened with Anna, I double checked on the other children and they are safe. Three of them are in South Molton and the eldest, Mary, is in Withypool."

"Do they know what he's done?"

"I don't think the youngest ones know, but I know for a fact that Mary knows, as she was at one of his inquests in Dulverton."

Thornton picked up his glass and after taking a sip, he looked into the fire and said, "Tell me, Superintendent, how can a man, locked in a cell, come by a pair of scissors, to do harm to himself?"

"That is a question I would like answered myself. I can only assume someone put them there in order for him to do as he intended. He didn't have them on him, as he was thoroughly searched, before he went into the cell."

"So, if one of the officers did that, why was he stopped?"

"I would assume, either the officer, who didn't put them there, overpowered Burgess and the culprit had to help or the other one would have got suspicious."

"Do you know which one?"

"No, and until someone says anything, we'll never know."

"Would have saved a costly trial, which is more than I can say about the contract for pumping out the mine."

"Yes. £250 I heard."

"Have you an idea of how long it will take?"

"A while I should imagine. But there's no hurry as the magistrate has remanded him until the winter assizes, which will be in December. So he isn't going anywhere. But if she isn't there, then there's no choice, but to let him go."

"She's there. I'm sure of it."

They finished their drinks and retired to bed.

In the next couple of weeks, work continued and the water was fast being reduced, but with rain pelting down and with the position of the mine, water still flowed in. Some of the machinery broke down and the pumps stopped. By the time the pumps resumed, the water level in the shaft had increased considerably again, adding valuable time to finding the body.

Eventually, in the middle of November, as the engineers were marking the water levels on a diagram of the shaft, a workman came running up to them and said, "The mine's empty!"

Skewes and Moffat ran over to the mineshaft and Skewes lay on the ground at the edge of the shaft. He breathed in through his nose and gave a look of disgust to Moffat and the workman. Getting up, he said, "The air's too foul to go down now. We'll have to leave it a while to dry out and if the smell doesn't go, we'll have to get some breathing equipment before we go down."

During the couple of days that followed, the engineers left the shaft to dry out. Meanwhile, not only did it rain, but water seeping down from the high ridges, flowed into the shaft again. When they looked into the shaft, the water level had risen and they had to re-start pumping. They told Jeffs and Goold that it would take another week to empty.

Disappointed, but not deterred, they agreed and Skewes and Moffat started straight away.

The length of time, which had elapsed since Anna's murder and the body still remaining undiscovered, sowed seeds of doubt in the public's mind whether at the approaching winter assizes – not withstanding his own confession of the crime – justice would be meted out to the murderer.

Jeffs was making a diligent search in the neighbourhood of the old mine and had occasionally referred, in glowing terms, to the tremendous efforts on the part of the contractors employed at intervals during the last three months in draining the large body of water out of the shafts and workings of the mine.

About a fortnight after it was found that the machinery had succeeded in pumping out nearly the whole of the water, because of an accumulation of foul air, the work was suspended, and water, again, rushed into the main shaft.

These and other serious difficulties, however, did not appal the courage of those engaged in the search, and so thoroughly convinced was Jeffs that the missing child would be found at the bottom of the main shaft, spurred on possibly by the near approach of the Somerset assizes, that, at this point, energies were redoubled, and prosecuted day by day with a zeal that must – if the surmise as to the place of concealment was correct – ensure success.

Then finally about half past six o'clock, on the morning of Thursday 2nd of December 1858, the water in the mine was reduced to within two feet of the bottom of the vertical shaft. At which time, Skewes descended the shaft to see that the pumps were in proper order, and upon reaching the bottom, he found a bag containing something bulky. He called the attention of his companion and partner, who was with him, to the discovery. Upon opening the bundle they found it was the corpse of a child.

Lodging the bag and its contents in one of the levels, they ascended the shaft, and communicated with police Constable Taylor, who was among the crowd and awaiting news. Skewes and Moffat then went down again, and having attached the bag to the windlass, it was drawn up. Constable Taylor grabbed hold of the bundle as it reached the top of the shaft; he untied the cord and placed the bundle on the ground. He then took out a knife and cut the twine. Cautiously he pulled the bundle apart and saw Anna's body. Taylor looked at it and at the sight of the body, turned and threw up.

When he regained a modicum of composure, he looked at the crowd and with a tear running down his face, said, "It's Anna Burgess."

He noticed the body was exceedingly clean but little decomposed, considering that it had been immersed in water at least four months. The little corpse, with portion of her wearing apparel still upon her, and a number of heavy stones, was wrapped up in an oil-skin coat. Taylor delicately enveloped Anna's body in the coat again and carried it to the blacksmith's shop at the cottage. He immediately put the body into a vessel containing water, so the body wouldn't decompose in the fresh air, and locked up the shop. Taylor then sent a message, along with the key to the shop, to Superintendent Jeffs, who at that time was in Exford, that the body had been found. He then made his way to Curry Rival to inform the coroner, Mr. William Munckton.

In the crowd at the mine, were a few reporters who, upon talking to Skewes and Moffat, found that the depth of the shaft was 216 feet, but that they found the body on a ledge 207 feet down from the edge of the main shaft.

When the Superintendent arrived at the mine, he unlocked the blacksmith's shop, opened the vessel, took out the bundle and looked at the body. In the inner sack he found two large stones, weighing about 22lbs. together; which had evidently being put in to sink the body. There were some clothes upon the child, and body and stones were enclosed in an old Macintosh coat, the inner bag was tied with a strong piece of cord.

Several medical gentlemen, John Barrett-Collyns and William Gaye, were soon in attendance to examine the body, along with some of the witnesses who had been examined before the magistrates at Dulverton. As soon as the body was exposed to view it was identified by Mrs. Marley and William Cockram, as that of the child, Anna Maria Burgess. Mrs. Marley also identified the black frock and other clothes upon the body as belonging to the deceased, and the Macintosh was recognised by both witnesses as having been worn by the prisoner, William Burgess.

On Saturday the 4th of December, at the 'White Horse Inn,' Exford, before Mr. W. W. Munckton, Esq., Coroner and after the jury had been sworn and charged as to their duties, they proceeded to the Wheal Eliza mine, Exmoor, which is about five miles from Exford, near Simonsbath, to view the body. It presented a horrid appearance. After the jury had seen the body, they returned to Exford and at two o'clock p.m. the inquest was resumed.

The first witness called was Thomas Skewes.

"I am Thomas Skewes," he said, "I am a mining engineer, and live at Molland, in Devonshire. In consequence of a contract with the magistrates of Dulverton division, about seven weeks ago, we commenced pumping out the water in the Wheal Eliza mine, situated in Exmoor Forest. On Thursday morning last, between half past six and seven o'clock, we got the water out to within a foot and a half of the bottom of the vertical shaft; about this time I went down, and John Moffatt, one of my partners, followed me.

"In the bottom of this shaft I saw a bag containing something. I took it up and placed it in one of the levels, about ten or twelve feet from the bottom; then I opened it in Moffatt's presence, to see what was in it. We saw that it contained the body of a child, and we brought it to the surface, and placed it in the hands of P.C. George Taylor, who was there assisting to pull it up. Soon afterwards it was placed in the smith's shop, close by the mine, and immersed in water, in a box, which was nailed down.

"The door was locked, and Taylor took away the key. I have seen the bag about this morning, when it was shown to the jury. I tore the bag with a piece of iron, and saw the body was wrapped up in another bag, and an oilcloth Macintosh. The bottom of the vertical shaft is thirty-six fathoms from the surface. There was a cord about the outside of the bag."

The next witness called was Constable George Taylor.

"I am George Taylor," he said, "I am a police constable, stationed at Exford. On Thursday morning last, I was present when last .witness and Moffatt went down in the Wheal Eliza mine, on Exmoor, at about seven o'clock. They called out to me that they had found something there containing a body. I directed them to bring it to the surface and I assisted them in doing so. In the course of a short time they brought up a bag containing an oil case coat, and the body of a child. There was a rope about the middle of the bag. It was taken to the blacksmith's shop and placed in a box filled with water, and I locked the door and took away the key. On Monday 16th August last, I received the piece of lilac cotton print, piece of black yarn stocking, and the piece of fur victorine, which I now produce, from Sarah Marley. On Wednesday the 18th of August, I went with Superintendent Jeffs to the allotment belonging to Mr. Mills, where the fire had been. I picked up several hooks and eyes, some fragments of tinder, and other things; they have been in my possession ever since."

The next witness called was Superintendent Jeffs.

"My name is Cresant Jeffs," he said, "I am Superintendent of the Somerset County police, Wiveliscombe division. From information which I received, at about half past ten o'clock on

Thursday morning last, I proceeded to the Wheal Eliza mine on Exmoor, and in a blacksmith's shop, near the mine, Thomas Skewes showed me a bag, immersed in water in a box. I opened the bag, and saw another bag of a coarser description, with a strong piece of cord tied round it near the centre. I cut the cord, and saw one of the legs, an arm, and the bottom part of the body of a child; close to its belly there were two large stones, weighing together 22lbs. About the body of the child was an oil case Macintosh. It has been under my charge at the blacksmith's shop ever since. This morning the jury, Mrs. Marley and others viewed it as I left.

"Then I placed it in charge of Messrs. Collyns and Gaye, surgeons. They stripped the body, and I here produced the clothes found upon it. From information which I received on Wednesday, the 18th of August last, I proceeded to Exmoor, and in a field, distant two fields from the back of the Red Deer Inn (Gallon House Inn), I found a spot where some female wearing apparel had been burned. I then went to a field where I was informed the prisoner had previously been at work; this field is about a mile distant from the field in which I found the remains of the clothes. There was a hole, which had the appearance of a grave; it was between three and four feet long and two feet wide in the centre, and about two to three feet deep. From other information I received, I commenced a search for the prisoner; I traced him to Lynmouth, in the county of Devon, and from thence to Swansea. I found him at work at the new docks now in course of erection there. I took him aside from the other men, and told him I wished to speak to him about his youngest daughter. He turned very pale, and appeared much confused, and said, "It's all right." I then told him I should arrest him on suspicion of murdering his child. He said, "I done it, and must die for it. I would sooner die than live; I shall never be happy no more." He then said, "My box that is at Exmoor I should like given to my second daughter, at North Molton; the money that is in my pocket and my clothes, you give to my boy." I then took him towards the police station at Swansea, and he repeated many times, "I would sooner die than live. I shall never be happy no more; I would have saved you the trouble to come and fetch me; I would have made away with myself, I ought to have done so before." He then said, "Have my other children seen it?" these remarks were quite voluntary on the part of the prisoner, and were not the consequence of my asking him questions. I searched him, and found two pound, six shillings, and a half a penny in his pockets, also the keys to his box."

Sarah Marley was called next.

"I am Sarah Marley," she said, "I am the wife of John Marley, of Gallon, or Red Deer Cottage, Exford. The 'Red Deer Inn' is opposite. At the Wheal Eliza mine, this morning the jury, viewed the remains of the body of Anna Maria Burgess, who was the daughter of William Burgess, a labourer. Both used to lodge with me. She was about six years old. I know her by her hair and clothes. She had brown straight hair.

"She came to lodge with me about the beginning of June last. On Saturday, the 24th of July last, the prisoner told me to clean her and get her clothes ready, as he was going to take her to Porlock, to his sister's. I cleaned the child and got her clothes ready; I put into a bundle one flannel petticoat, three cotton frocks, one of lilac colour, one brown or chocolate colour, and one a light colour with stripes in it, and a fur victorine; these were tied up in a cotton handkerchief. The prisoner left the pinafore, part of which is now produced, with me on the 10th August. The child had two pinafores of the pattern now produced by P.C. George Taylor."

She was shown a piece of burnt cotton print of lilac colour.

"Yes. That is of the same colour and pattern as the child's pinafore. The piece of fur produced is of the same description of material as the petticoat I put in the bundle; there was also tied up in the bundle of clothes two pairs of black yarn stockings of the same pattern as the piece produced. The child had one pair of boots, and I bought the only pair of shoes she had off the prisoner on the morning of the 10th of August. I was in the habit of lacing up or tying her boots, as she could not do it herself; I did this for her every day; I have examined the boots now produced by Superintendent Jeffs, and I believe that they are the same boots she had on when she left. The child did not return on the Sunday evening. A few days after the prisoner returned to my house; I asked him whether there were many children where the child was, and he replied, "Yes, but she is not going to stay there long." The prisoner paid for its maintenance regular; he once told me he thought half a crown was too much, but I told him I did not think it was. I told him I would keep her and use her as a child of my own, if he would leave her with me. The prisoner returned to my house about three o'clock on Sunday 25th of July. The Macintosh now produced belonged to William Burgess; I know it by the dark blue cloth collar. The things now shown me by Superintendent Jeffs belonged to the deceased.

"The shift I know by the pattern and make, and there is some of my work about it; and it was the only one she had. The woollen jacket and the black stuff frock I know, the latter by a place in the skirt, which I sewed up. The stuff petticoat had been an old frock. All these garments, with the exception of the shift, she had on when I last saw her alive. I washed and mended the shift and placed it in Burgess's bedroom for the deceased to put on the Sunday she left. On Tuesday, the 27th of July last, I saw Burgess wearing the Macintosh. William Cockram lodges with me, and used to sleep with William Burgess. He did so on the night of 24th day of July last. He sold me a pair of shoes, which belonged to deceased for nine pence, when he left."

William Cockram was the next witness called.

"I am William Cockram; I live at Exford, in the county of Somerset, and I am a labourer. I lodged with the prisoner during the month of July last, at a cottage situate near the Gallon House, in the parish of Exford. I slept in the same bed with the prisoner; on Sunday, the 25th of July, the prisoner turned out of his bed at half-past three o'clock in the morning. He said, "William, will you please tell me what time it is?" He unhung my watch, which was hanging by the side of the bed, and handed it to me; I looked at the watch and saw it was half-past three. The prisoner dressed himself and went downstairs; he did not say where he was going. The prisoner's daughter Anna aged six years, slept in the same bed with us; after he had dressed himself, he said to his daughter, "Anna, come, turn out," the child got up, and left the room with him. I saw the prisoner again on the evening of the same day, between nine and ten o'clock, in our lodgings; he was in the bed that I sleep in. I have not seen the child since; she did not return with him. The Macintosh about the body belonged to William Burgess; he wore it on the 27th of July last. The deceased's hair was cut short behind and about her ears."

Mary Farley was called next.

"I am Mary Farley, I am a single woman, and live at Gallon House cottage, in the parish of Exford. On Sunday the 15th of August, I went up to Mr. Mills' allotment to see where the fire had been, and I there picked up a piece of lilac cotton print, and a piece of a black yarn stocking. I know the bit of print as a piece of Anna Burgess's pinafore; I had seen it at Sarah Marley's, because I had washed there. I have washed the pinafore; I took the things I picked up to Sarah Marley's with whom the child had been living. I asked her if she knew it, and she said, "Yes, it is a piece of Anna Burgess's pinafore." I saw the prisoner about six weeks ago, when he said, "I am going to leave the country." I said, "Not you," prisoner replied, "I be." I said, "Where are you going to – be you going to take the little maid with you?"

The prisoner replied, "Yes, I be."."

The surgeon Dr. Collyns was called next.

"I am John Barrett-Collyns; I am a surgeon, residing at Dulverton. I have today made a post mortem examination of a female child, which the jury viewed this morning at the Wheal Eliza mine on Exmoor. Mr. Gaye, of Williton, and Dr. Sydenham assisted me. It was placed under my charge, with the coverings, by Superintendent Jeffs. The body was enclosed in a coarse hempen sack externally, and a black Macintosh internally; a rope was tied around the Macintosh, corresponding to the upper part of the body. Clothes covered the body, and were huddled; a Spencer with long sleeves, black stuff frock with short sleeves, a brown stuff petticoat with check lining, and a white shift; a pinkish plain shawl, folded, was tied around the chest, below the arms over the frock, in a knot placed behind. Black earth and gravel, with particles of slate, were diffused generally about the dress and exposed parts of the body. Several lumps of the soil before described were found underneath the shawl; its outer surface was generally free from it. I removed these coverings and articles of dress and delivered them to Superintendent Jeffs. The whole of the body was much decomposed, and sodden from maceration. The body was crumpled up, the legs being flexed upon the trunk, the head reclining on the right shoulder, with the left arm and hand raised around it. The right arm was flexed, with the back of the hand against the head. The hair was brown, longer in front than behind, where it appeared to have been cut evenly round. The tip of the tongue protruded slightly between the teeth, which were perfect, and clenched, leaving their impressions upon the tongue; the nose was flattened, but the bones were unbroken and not displaced. On raising the head, the right ear and a portion of the scalp adjoining were found lacerated, and a fracture of the skull beneath was visible. On opening the head, the *dura mater* was still firm. It was torn on the right side, corresponding to the seat of the fracture. The fracture extended across the centre of the base of the skull, and was about four inches in length. The brain was very much decomposed, and presented a pinker hue at the base than elsewhere. In the large vein of the *dura mater*, a light drab thickish fluid was found, but not to be recognised as blood. The skin under the angle of the jaw on the right side was livid, the cellular tissue beneath it infiltrated with a thin layer of a dark substance, and the *masseter muscle* adjoining partook of the same discolouration. The muscles of the neck contiguous to the wind pipe were relatively little decomposed and uninjured. A notable mark, as of a bruise, was apparent on the skin over the central part of the breast-bone, extending somewhat to the left, and involved the soft parts underneath. On opening the chest about half a pint of bloody fluid was found in the sac covering each lung; both lungs appeared to be congested, and were generally emphysematous, the latter condition arising most likely from decomposition. The sac of the heart contained also a small quality of bloody fluid. The right side of the heart contained thick decomposed blood; the left side was empty. The entrails were escaping from the belly. All the viscera appeared healthy. The liver and spleen were unusually pale in colour, probably from maceration. The stomach contained partially digested food, and the bladder was empty. I should think the child was about six- or seven-years of age. She appeared to have died in good condition. I believe the fracture of the skull to have been caused during life, by a direct blow against the side of the head from behind, and implicating the right ear. Such a fracture would, in all probability, cause death, but not immediately. From the appearances on the surface of the chest, and the state of the lungs and heart within, I infer that pressure was made during life on the chest, which pressure would hasten death. Death would still further be accelerated by covering over the mouth and nostrils, so as to exclude the passage of air. From all the appearances, I am of the opinion that the immediate cause of death was suffocation. The stomach contained partially digested food, consisting of meat and potatoes. I think the fracture would be caused by the body being thrown into the mine after death. I am of the opinion that the child, in her dress, had been interred, and that the folded shawl, which was tied around it, was placed there after it had been taken up again."

The next witness was William Thomas Gaye.

"I am William Gaye," he said, "I am a surgeon, residing at Williton. I corroborate Mr. Collyns evidence in its entire extent. When he stepped down Superintendent Jeffs was re-examined and said, "At the pit resembling a grave, spoken of in my former evidence, on 'Picked Stones,' the soil is of dark colour, resembling the earth which I saw about the clothes found on the deceased, especially under the shawl spoken of by Mr. Collyns. Beneath this soil is gravel and skillet mixed with a slatey substance."

When Jeffs stood down, the coroner looked at all the evidence before him and asked the jury to retire to find their verdict. When the jury returned, their verdict was WILFUL MURDER AGAINST WILLIAM BURGESS.

The coroner issued his warrant of detainer to the Governor of Taunton Gaol, where Burgess was confined.

It was nine o'clock at night when the inquiry ended and the coroner and the jury spoke in the highest possible terms of the persevering exertions of Superintendent Jeffs, but for whom, in all human probability, the case might have been for ever enshrouded in mystery.

Chapter Thirteen

Straight after the inquest, Anna's body was taken from the blacksmith shop at the mine to her final resting place at St. Luke's Church in Simonsbath. The whole village turned out see her being buried, but the one person not there was her father, who was sitting in his cell, waiting for the trial at the winter assizes on the 20th of December.

On the morning of the 20th, shortly after nine o'clock, the approaches to the crown court were crowded with people anxious to secure the best places in the court to hear the trial. The greatest order and decorum prevailed, not withstanding the intense interest the case appeared to have excited.

At precisely ten o'clock, His lordship, Sir John Barnard Byles, entered the court and when Burgess stepped up to the box, the buzz of conversation among the audience was succeeded by breathless silence, and all eyes were turned towards Burgess. He was wearing the same clothes, since he appeared before the magistrates in Dulverton.

Forty-nine-year-old William Karslake and eighty-three-year-old Richard Meade King were the council for the prosecution and Mr. Rotten, (I could find no information on this person) had been assigned by the judge to undertake to watch the case on his behalf. Forty-five-year-old, Mr. Henry C. Trenchard was acting as Burgess's defence.

Burgess was arraigned on an indictment which charged him with wilful murder of Anna Maria Burgess; and was asked by the Clerk of Assizes, Mr. Gurney, (again no information was found on this person) whether he was guilty or not guilty.

Burgess replied, "Not guilty, your honour."

Gurney further asked if when indicted for the murder on the coroner's inquest, how he pleaded. Burgess again replied, "Not guilty, sir."

Before Burgess was given in charge to the jury, Mr. Rotton said, "I appear, my lord, by the kindness of the court to watch this case on the part of the prisoner, and I think it right at this stage to say to the gentlemen in the box, that if there be any amongst them to form a judgement upon it, I hope, in justice to the prisoner, they will leave the box and let other gentlemen be sworn in their place.

Judge Byles answered, "I think that somewhat irregular."

Mr. Rotton shrugged and said, "Go through your challenges in the usual way."

The jury were then sworn without any juror being challenged, either on the part of the Crown or of the prisoner.

Mr. Karslake opened the case in a careful and temperate address. He said, "The indictment, which has been read informed the jury of the nature of the charge made against the prisoner; and I am quite sure that, the charge being of so grave a character, you would give, as you are bound to do, your most serious and anxious attention to it. The prisoner standing indicted for the crime of wilful murder – murder committed on his own helpless child; and I could not conceal from myself that the case had created throughout the county very great excitement indeed. Probably its details had been canvassed in their presence; and they had, as they had a perfect right to do, expressed their opinions upon it, hostile or otherwise, to the prisoner at the bar."

Karslake looked at the jury momentarily and continued, "I am, however, well aware of the duty you have to perform; and as it had fallen to you to be impanelled for the purpose of trying this most serious case, you will discard from your minds everything you have heard beyond the walls of the court; and I am confident that upon the evidence, which I, by the assistance of my learned friend, would be able to place before you and upon that evidence alone you will pronounce your verdict. It is unnecessary for me to do anything more than state succinctly and clearly the circumstances of the case; and I ask your careful attention, not only to the general details, but to the minute circumstances which might become important hereafter."

He walked to the box and looked at Burgess, sitting there silently and as he looked at Burgess, he said, "The charge is, as I have said, that the prisoner – being, as the law presumed, a person of sound mind and competent understanding – had, of malice aforethought, committed the crime of murder upon his own child; and," he turned to the jury, "when I ask you to look at the minute details, it was in order that you might see whether the scheme, which the prisoner had laid in his own mind, had not been carried out by him with fraud and subtlety and determination, showing that he was perfectly conscious of the act which he committed.

"The prisoner has for many years been working at Exmoor, and was a native of Porlock. He was occasionally employed by different farmers and gentlemen, but for the last couple of years he was principally occupied in mining operations – there being, as the jury are aware, several mines in the district, and a considerable quantity of minerals raised. He lived at a house called Gallon House cottage, immediately opposite a public house called Gallon House Inn, which was also called the Red Deer.

"On the 24th of July the prisoner was living at the cottage, and for about three weeks previously, the child whom he is accused of having murdered lived with him. The child was about six-years of age, and was the only one that was maintained by the prisoner, who was a widower.

"The child was placed under the care of a Sarah Marley, to whom the prisoner paid 2s 6d a week for her maintenance; and small as that sum was, he appeared to have paid it unwillingly and grudgingly. On more than one occasion he asked Mrs. Marley to take a less sum per week, but she refused; and up to the day in question the prisoner paid the amount which he had agreed. On the 24th of July the prisoner gave instructions to Mrs. Marley to have the child cleaned, in order that he might taker her away to his sister, or some relative, living in Porlock.

"Accordingly Mrs. Marley prepared the child for the journey on the following morning. The child went to bed, and slept in the same room as the prisoner; and he left the next morning at half-past-three, stating it was his intention to go to Porlock – a little town on the channel, about seven miles distant from the Gallon House, across the moor. From that moment the child was never seen alive again."

Karslake walked to the table with where his notes were and quickly scanned the documents, then turned back to the jury and said, "In which direction the prisoner went, I do not pretend to say; but certainly between three and four o'clock he left, and at half-past-seven or eight o'clock he arrived at his brother-in-law's house at Porlock, without the child. He was in a wet state; but this might be accounted for by the fact that it rained during the morning and going across the moor, he was probably overtaken by the storm. He returned the same afternoon to the cottage, and remained there until the 10th of August. In the course of that time, reference was made to the poor child on more than one occasion, and he said that she has gone to live with his relatives. He was asked were there any children, that the child could play with, and he said that there were not many children, and he spoke of the child repeatedly as being still in existence.

"On the 10th of August he left the Gallon House cottage, and said he was going to seek work elsewhere; and from that time my learned council could give no account of him till a later period, to which he should refer by and by, when he was found in Swansea, and taken in custody for the murder of the child.

"Previously to this, a considerable suspicion had arisen that the child had been unfairly dealt with; and upon an enquiry made at Porlock, it was ascertained that she had not been left with the prisoner's relatives there and a search was instituted; and at no distance from the cottage, it was discovered that a fire had been kindled and among the embers were the remains of certain clothes, which beyond all question, had belonged to the murdered child.

"When the child left the house with the prisoner, all her little wardrobe was made up in a bundle by Mrs. Marley, by the prisoners orders and that Mrs. Marley tells us what clothes were put into that bundle, and would identify some of the things that were found in the embers of the fire as having belonged to the unfortunate child. Suspicions were thus increased, but no tidings of the child could be obtained; and it was certain that the prisoner's statement that he had taken her to Porlock was untrue.

"Accordingly the superintendent of police proceeded to Lynmouth, and from there he went to Swansea, where he found the prisoner, and at once charged him with the murder. He admitted that he had done it and he did not appear to know whether the body had been found or not, but he seemed to be overtaken with the pangs of conscience, and stated that if the superintendent had not come to him, he should have made away with himself. The prisoner then gave to the officers certain directions what was to be done with the money he had upon him, and the box which he had left at the cottage; and upon his carpetbag being searched, there was found a pair of children's boots, which would be identified as those that were worn by the unfortunate child on the morning of the 25th of July."

Karslake, again looked at his notes and took a sip of water, then said, "After the prisoner was in custody, further enquiries were made, and a search was instituted in every direction, for the purpose of finding the body. At a place close to where the prisoner had been working, a small trench was found, having the appearance of a grave, near a hedge. I am not saying that the child's body was placed there; but under the circumstances there would be little doubt that it was temporary buried there, and afterwards dug up again by the prisoner and put in the shaft of the old Wheal Eliza mine. This mine was one of the mines the prisoner used to work and knew it was disused. The shafts had in consequence become completely filled with water and that the shaft was 216 feet deep. After the prisoner was in custody, and had been taken more than once before the magistrates at Dulverton, the magistrates, having reason to suspect that the body had been cast into this deserted mine, most kindly came forward, and for purposes of having it searched, the water was pumped out at a considerable expense. A contract was taken on the 14th of October and on the 2nd of December the water had been cleared out, when the bottom of that deep shaft the body of the unfortunate child was found."

Karslake stopped, looked at the prisoner, then the jury and then the crowd and after a moment where he just stared at the crowd, said, "It now became necessary to state in what condition it was found, how it was dressed, and in what way it was wrapped up for the purpose of being disposed of."

He looked back to the jury and continued, "The body was in a sack and a second sack was placed over that. The sacks were tied round with a rope, and upon further investigation it seemed that around the body there was a Macintosh tightly wrapped. This is a fact which it was most important to remember, for it belonged to the prisoner at the bar, and he was seen with it on two days after the 25th of July. Two heavy stones were placed in it for the purpose of assisting to sink the body, and the child was dressed in the clothes which Mrs. Marley had placed for her to use when she left the cottage; but the boots were missing and these as I have already explained, were found in the prisoner's bag in Swansea. It appeared that there was also a shawl placed round the body, under the Macintosh; and under the shawl there were large pieces of earth, which had evidently been upon the child's person at the time the Macintosh was wrapped round it. It was a curious and remarkable fact, that the soil thus found corresponds with that which was found in the vicinity of the grave; and it seemed most probable that, having made up his mind to murder the poor child, the prisoner put the body into this grave as a temporary precaution, but ultimately removed it from that resting place, and threw it into the shaft, where for the expenditure of a large sum of money, and the accidental circumstances of that particular shaft being searched, for there were many other shafts around, it might never have come to light. The witness I will call, will, I believe, no doubt upon the minds of the jury that the prisoner's hand committed the murder and I think there will be no question that the crime was planned before he left, on the 25th of July, even more so, the day before, when he gave his directions to Mrs. Marley. Whether he murdered the child immediately, I cannot tell, or whether he went in the direction of Porlock; but certainly the child was missed on the 25th of July, and the body was found on the 2nd of December as I have described."

Karslake walked back to his table, took another sip of water and as he lifted his head to drink, he looked about the crowd and saw an old woman, who, although it was cold, she looked pale and slowly passed the fan she was waving in front of her face. When he placed the glass on the table he turned to face the jury, still keeping an eye on the woman, and said, "One word as to the post mortem examination that had been made. It showed that the child did not come to its end from drowning, but marks of considerable violence, sufficient to account for death, were traced on the body, notwithstanding the long time it had been in the water." He looked at the old woman, who was fanning more quickly, a small grin appeared on his face and continued, "On the side of the head there was a severe fracture of the skull; and the surgeons were of an opinion, that the injury was sustained during life. The nose was flattened; the tongue was protruding through the lips, and the teeth tightly clenched upon it."

A shriek came from the crowd and when everybody looked towards the noise, they saw the old lady collapsed on the floor. Some people picked her up and as everybody looked in the woman's direction, Karslake smiled, his plan had worked and his narration of the procedures had grabbed the crowd's attention.

When everything settled, Karslake continued, "It was apparent that the child had sustained considerable violence, and this had occasioned corresponding internal injuries. The surgeons would give it, as their opinion, that the child was first struck a violent blow in the head, by which the skull was fractured, and after that death was caused by suffocation, by means of pressure upon the chest. It might be asked what was the prisoner's motive? It is not for me to go in search of motives; I do not know what motives might have actuated him; but it seemed that he grudged the pittance paid for the maintenance of the unfortunate child; and whether his object was to get rid of that small payment, I do not know. But I understand that some questions would be raised as to whether he was sane; if that was the case the jury will hear the evidence upon which is rested. All I can say is, that you must look into all circumstances of the case, and see whether there had not been a plan, and whether the prisoner, in acting out his dreadful design, had not shown that he was quite competent to know the nature of the act he was performing; I ask you however painful the duty, to say whether or not, beyond all doubt, the crime was brought home to the prisoner."

The Wheal Eliza Murder

Chapter Fourteen

When the court had settled, Mr. Karslake called his first witness. The first witness was Thomas Skewes. When he sat in the witness box, Karslake said, "Mr. Skewes, can you tell me what your job is and how you are connected to this case?"

"I have been employed for many years as a mining engineer, and live at Molland, Devon," Skewes replied. "In October last I was employed by the magistrates to pump out water of the wheal Eliza Mine, Exmoor."

"Can you tell the court," Karslake asked, "when you started this work and what you found."

"I began on the 16th of October; the mine had been worked and then discontinued and the shafts and adits became full of water. I took the contract for the pumping out the water for this search for £250. I got out the water by the 2nd of December. The depth of the shaft was 215 feet and there were many adits leading to it, full of water. On the 2nd of December when we were about eighteen inches of water left, I went down with one of my partners and found a bag, which appeared to have something in it. The mouth of the bag lapped over, and a cord was tied round to make it fast. I took it up ten or twelve feet to a level above. I then made further examination and I slipped the outside bag and found another bag inside and inside the inner bag there was an old Macintosh coat. Constable Taylor was at the top of the shaft. We then brought it up and delivered it to him. On inspection, Constable Taylor found the body of the child."

"Did you see the body?" Karslake asked.

"Not at first, but I did when myself and my partner got out of the shaft."

"So if you didn't see the body," Karslake said, "how did you know it was a child?"

"I had felt it, the bag, before we got it up."

"Then what happened?"

"I left the body in charge of Constable Taylor, who put it in the old blacksmith's shop at the mine and it was put in water."

"Do you know the prisoner? And do you know Porlock?" Mr. Rotton asked him.

"I don't know anything about Porlock, except it's on the coast and I do not know the prisoner and have never seen him before."

Karslake looked at Mr. Rotton, who in turn shook his head. Karslake turned to the judge and said, "No more questions, your honour."

When Skewes left the box, Karslake called for the next witness, George Taylor.

"My name is George Taylor," he said, "I am a police constable at Exford, and I was present at the Wheal Eliza mine with the last witness on the 2nd of December."

"Can you tell the court," Karslake said, "what you saw?"

"I saw something be brought up from the bottom of the shaft and when I examined it, it was the body of a child."

"And what did you do?"

"I had it put in a box full of water and nailed down and removed it to the blacksmith's shop, where it was locked up and I took the key."

Karslake nodded to a man and said, "Do you recognise this item?"

The man picked up an old Macintosh coat and held it up for Taylor to see.

Taylor looked at it and replied, "The Macintosh which has been produced is the one in which the body was wrapped."

"Do you recognise these items?"

The man held up two bags and Taylor said, "Yes. The outside and inner bags, in which the body was in."

The man held up a shawl and jacket and Taylor answered, "The plaid shawl produced was tied round the waist and the jacket was tied round the body."

"Can you tell me about these items?" Karslake asked and the man held up some items. Taylor looked at them and said, "Yes, the black frock, petticoat and shift was on the body."

The man held up a two pieces of rope and Taylor said, "The larger rope was tied round the body and the smaller one was tied round the Macintosh."

Karslake took hold of the rope, turned to the jury and crowd, and demonstrated how the rope had been tied by sliding noose tied round the top of the Macintosh and the two pieces were part of the same rope. When he had finished his demonstration, he turned back to Taylor and asked, "These were the only clothing on the body, were they not?"

"Yes. The child had no boots on her feet," Taylor replied.

"And what did you do with the child's clothing?"

"I took them off the body on the day. Mr. Jeffs was present when I saw them on the 2nd and I produced the remains of a blue lilac pinafore, a piece of flannel petticoat, a black stocking, part of a victorine, a bit of frock, another piece of lilac print, which were all burnt, also a quantity of tinder, and hooks and eyes."

"These pieces of clothing and the hooks and eyes? Where did you find them?" asked Karslake.

"I got the pieces from Sarah Marley on the 16th of August. I found the hooks and eyes in an allotment belonging to Mr. Mills, near the Gallon House Cottage. These things have been in my possession ever since."

Karslake looked at Rotton, who nodded and stood up. He looked at Taylor and asked, "Did you know the prisoner, before?"

"Yes. I have known the prisoner for 18 months before this, I knew he was much given to drinking and I have seen him drunk on many occasion. I believe he was in regular work and got about 12 shillings a week."

"Did you know the child?" Rotton asked.

"I knew the deceased child, but I never saw him with her and I do not know what his conduct was towards her."

Karslake then stood up and asked, "Do you know where he worked?"

Taylor watched Rotton sit down and answered, "During the eighteen months I knew him, he worked at mining on 'Picked Stones,' near the Gallon House."

"What was his attitude when he was drinking?" Karslake asked.

"When he was drunk he was very violent and disorderly," replied Taylor.

Rotton stood up and asked, "How was his attitude different to other people in the village, when drunk?"

Taylor looked strangely at Rotton and replied, "He was much the same as other men are when drunk, but very well in his behaviour when sober."

Karslake looked at Rotton, who shook his head, and sat down. Karslake then turned back to Taylor and told him to step down and called the next witness, who was Superintendent Jeffs.

When Jeffs took the stand, he said, I am Cresant Jeffs. I am Superintendent of police at Wiveliscombe.

"Superintendent, do you recognise the items on display?" Karslake asked.

"Yes. The clothes produced are the same I saw on the body of Anna Maria Burgess."

The judge interrupted and said to Karslake, "We have now confirmed that the items on show are the clothes the child was wearing and now that we have that confirmed by three witnesses, I suggest we move them from the court, before we are overcome by the stench."

"Yes, Your Honour, I agree."

With that the man took up the clothes and removed them from the court and then the sheriff had the passages sprinkled with disinfectant and when the air was breathable again, Karslake continued questioning Jeffs.

"I went to the Wheal Eliza mine on the 2nd of December and the body had been put in water, the bags were still round the body. I opened the bags and took out the Macintosh. I opened it and in the skirts of the Macintosh, I found two large stones, weighing about 22lbs. I saw the remnants of some more clothes at the bottom."

"Were you present at the post mortem?" Karslake asked.

"Yes. I was present at the post mortem examination on the 4th of December and it was made by Mr. Collyns and Mr. Gaye. There was some slate and black earth inside and underneath the shawl tied round the body, and some on top between the shawl and Macintosh, but only a little. It was dark soil – shallet, or rotten slate stuff."

"Can you tell the court of the events leading to you finding the prisoner?"

"On the 18th of August I saw a place called 'Picked Stones', I examined the shallet with the soil at the spot. The soil I found about the clothes of the child was of the same description. In consequence of suspicions I entertained, on the same day; I went to the Gallon House, Exmoor and observed a place where some burnt clothes had been found. The place is called 'Mills' allotment'. I found in the embers some hooks and eyes, and some burnt tinder. I had known this part of the country before and the high road from Exford to Porlock would be four miles further than going across the forest. The moor is accessible to foot passengers. In consequence of information I had received, I went to Lynmouth in search of the prisoner there. I reached Lynmouth on the night of the 18th of August and I did not find the prisoner there. In consequence of what I heard, I went to Swansea and found him working in the docks there, excavating. I went up to him and called him to one side. I had some conversation with him and I held out no enticement to him to say anything. I said, "Burgess, I want to speak to you about your youngest daughter." He turned very pale, and looked much confused and he then said, "It's all right"."

At that moment Burgess, who seemed comparatively calm, became exceedingly violent. Striking the front of the dock with peculiar vehemence of manner and said to the witness, "You're a liar. You never said any such thing."

"Be quiet, Prisoner!" shouted the judge.

"I sha'nt," Burgess shouted back then looked at Jeffs and shouted, "The bee'st a liar. I never said such thing, you nasty devil."

The officers of the court tried to induce him to keep offence, but in vain, and Burgess, raising his arms above his head and flourishing it at the same time, exclaimed, "You never said any such thing to me. If I am to lose my life at once. You devil."

Jeffs continued, "I then told the prisoner, I should arrest him on suspicion of murdering his child. He replied, "I did it, and must die for it.""

"And so I will," Burgess shouted.

"I would, he then said," Jeffs continued, "sooner die than live, for I shall never be happy anymore"."

Burgess violently shouted, "That's a lie! But I'll suffer the law between you all; of course I don't want to live. I bea'nt drunk now, but I have had no drink lately; they wouldn't let me; and if I never have say, I should not be here now."

When Burgess settled down, Jeffs continued with his testimony, "I took the prisoner into custody, he said, "My box that is at Exmoor I should like given to my second daughter at South molton and the money that is in my pocket and my clothes, you give to my boy." He also said, "I would have saved you the trouble to come to fetch me, I would have made away with myself, I ought to have done so before." I took him to the station at Swansea. I also when with him to his lodgings and searched them. I found there the pair of boots produced. On the 21st of August at Dulverton, I took the boots out of a bag in the prisoner's presence. He said, "they are a pair of boots I bought for my boy." I showed those boots to Sarah Marley, and also to William Smith."

Karslake sat down and Rotton stood up and asked, "Do you know where the prisoner's sister lives?"

"No. I was not acquainted with the neighbourhood of Porlock."

"When the prisoner was brought back from Swansea, where did you take him?" asked Rotton.

"I took him to Simonsbath and then to Dulverton."

"Can you tell me what happened at Dulverton?"

"I gave him to P.C. Taylor at Dulverton and I believe he made an attempt on his life," Jeffs replied.

"Do you know anything about the prisoner's family?"

"I do not know anything of the prisoner's family. I made inquiries but did not ascertain anything positive about them."

Rotton sat back down and shook his head at Karslake, who told the witness to step down.

When Jeffs left the witness box, Karslake called John Barrett-Collyns to the box, who when asked replied, "I am a surgeon living in Dulverton, where I have been in practice since 1845. I made the post mortem examination of the body of a child at the Wheal Eliza Mine on the 4th of December, Mr. Gaye was present. The body was given into my charge by Mr. Jeffs. The body was wrapped in a hempen sack externally and in that a Macintosh. I observed soil on the clothes, and on the exposed parts of the body; there was comparatively little on the shawl tied round the body.

"Underneath the shawl and beneath the frock there were several lumps of soil. The body was generally decomposed and sodden of maceration, as through being in the water some time. The body was crumpled up together; the legs were flexed forward; the head was reclining on the right shoulder, with the left arm and hand raised up, and the right arm with the back of the hand against the head. The tongue was protruding slightly between the teeth, which were perfect and clenched, and left their impression upon it. The nose was flattened, but the bones of her face were not broken. The scalp was in an adipose state. The hair was longer in front than behind, where it appeared to have been cut evenly round. There was a fracture of the skull on the right side extending down to the canal of the ear and across the base of the skull. I observed an appearance of laceration corresponding with that fracture. The scalp was torn at that part. Internally I found a corresponding fracture. It might in my judgement have been caused by a heavy blunt instrument. I am of the opinion, from the appearance, that the fracture was inflicted during life, by a blow from behind. On the brain there was an absence of effusion of blood, which would be accounted for by the long time the body had been in the water. I opened a large vein, but the fluid did not appear to be blood. I found an external contusion on the breast bone, and I observed that the discolouration more or less extended down to the knee. A portion of the cellular tissue was discoloured. The sac covering of the lungs contained about half a pint of bloody fluid each. The lungs themselves appeared to have been congested. The sac of the heart also contained some bloody fluid. The right side of the heart contained some portions of blood, and the left side was empty."

At that moment a man got up and rushed out of the court and could be heard throwing up in the passage.

Collyns continued, "The abdominal viscera were generally healthy. There were in the stomach portions of undigested food – meat and potatoes."

Another person, a young woman, got up quickly and also rushed out of the court to vomit.

"The appearance of the chest," Collyns continued, "was the result of pressure or from smothering. They would indicate generally that death had resulted from suffocation. The appearance of the tongue and marks of the teeth on it would support that opinion. The internal appearance of the chest must have been caused by external pressure during life."

"Had you know the prisoner before this tragic incident?" Karslake asked.

"Yes," Collyns replied, "I had known the prisoner and his family, and I attended his child, but not the deceased. I believe he lost his wife some time ago."

Mr. Rotton asked, "In your opinion on how the child was murdered."

"It was possible the death might have immediately ensued from the fracture. The flattening of the nose might have been result of the pressure after death by the Macintosh and sack, in which the body was enveloped. Supposing it had ensued from the blow, there might have been some appearance on the chest from pressure. It might have been the same appearance on the lungs."

"You stated you knew the prisoner, before hand," Rotton asked, "Exactly how long have you known the prisoner?"

"I have known the prisoner for three years. His wife was living when I knew him."

"What was your opinion on their family life?" Rotton asked.

"He was generally kind to his family, so far as I know," Collyns replied.

"What were you generally called out for, regarding the Burgess family?"

"Not really a lot. In September 1855, I attended his boy, who was ten or twelve years old, when he met with an accident."

"Thank you. No more questions," said Rotton and sat down.

Karslake stood up and asked Collyns, "Can you tell me again about the bruise on the chest."

Collyns looked at Karslake strangely and replied, "Coupling the injuries to the chest, and the appearance of the teeth and tongue, I am of the opinion the bruise was inflicted during life."

"Thank you, Dr. Collyns," Karslake said. "You may step down. And I call Mr. Gaye."

When Collyns had sat down and Gaye was sitting in the box, Karslake asked him his opinion with the post mortem and Gaye replied, "On the 4th of December I assisted in the post mortem examination of the child and I fully agree with what the evidence that Dr. Collyns had given and I know nothing more."

Mr. Rotton stood up and asked him if he had met the prisoner before and Gaye replied, "I do not know the prisoner, but I believe I know a first cousin of his."

Rotton looked at him and said, "No more questions."

Karslake told him to step down and called Sarah Marley to the stand.

The Wheal Eliza Murder

Chapter Fifteen

"I am Sarah Marley," she said, "I am the wife of John Marley, and live at the Gallon House Cottage, Exford. Some time ago the prisoner came to lodge at my house."

Karslake asked, "Can you tell me when he came to your house?"

"I believe it was the beginning of June last. He had lodged with me once about twelve months before."

"Did you know how he made his living?"

"He got his living by working at the mines of Exmoor."

"You said he lived with you once before, did he have the child with him then?"

"No."

"Did he move in this time with the child?"

"He had been living with me some time before he brought the child."

"How long was the child staying at your house?"

"She had been with me about three weeks, when she left on the 25th of July.

"Did you know how old she was when she moved in?"

"She was about six years old."

"How much did he pay you?"

"He arranged to pay me half-a-crown a week."

"Was that for him and the child?"

"I told him if he gave me half-a-crown a week, I would keep her as if she were my own."

"And you agreed on that amount?"

"Yes. We agreed on half-a-crown a week."

"And when she left, did he want to change the amount?"

"The last week he paid me, he asked if I should charge him the same, I said yes."

"When did he last pay you rent?"

"He paid the last money a few days after he took away the child."

"When was the last time you saw the child?"

"On the 24th of July, to the evening, he told me to clean her and get her clothes ready, as he was going to take her to Porlock to his sister's. I cleaned the child and got her clothes ready; I did so and saw the child go into his bed-room to go to bed; she slept in the same room with him and a man called Cockram. I prepared a shift for her to put on, on the Sunday morning. I had put all her clothes ready in the prisoner's room."

"When he told you he was taking the child away, was this the only time he said that?"

"No. He told me a week before that he was going, but he did not get up so early as he wanted on the Sunday morning. I said to him, "You ain't gone!" and the prisoner said, "No; I shall leave it a week longer.""

"What did you put in the bundle, which the prisoner took with him?"

"On the 24th of July, I tied up the things in a cotton handkerchief. I put into the bundle one flannel petticoat, three cotton frocks, a fur victorine, and two pair of yarn stockings."

"And what did you put out for the child to wear on her journey to her auntie's house?"

"The child had on a black frock, and a brown petticoat, stockings, and little boots, when I saw her last on the Saturday. She had no shift, besides the one I put in her room for her to put on, on the Sunday morning."

"But you never saw her on the Sunday morning as she left?"

"No. I did not see the child alive after that Saturday night."

"But she did go?"

"When I got up I found the prisoner and the child were gone."

"And when did you see the prisoner again?"

"He came back again about three in the afternoon. The child was not with him. I said, "How is your mother?" He said, "She fo'near the same, and will never be any better in the world." I had talked to him before about his mother being ill."

"Did you mention the child after she had gone?"

"A few days after, I asked him if there were any more children, where the little maid was, and he said, "Yes, but she is not going to stay there long." The money was due to me when he took away the child, but he did not pay me till a few days afterwards. He said, "Are you going to charge me the same, and I said, "Yes." He then paid me half-a-crown, that is, a week for the child, and a week for himself."

"What date did you know that the prisoner had moved out?"

"On the 10th of August, he left me altogether; he left a box and several things at my house; he sold me a little pair of shoes the same morning he left."

"And whose shoes were they?"

"Anna's."

"How did you know they were hers?"

"Anna Maria Burgess had been in the habit of wearing them."

"Did he say where he was going?"

"He did not say where he was going. I asked a question a few days before and he said, "He shouldn't resolve any one where he was going. He asked whether the shoes would be any use to me, and I gave him 9d for them."

"How many pairs of shoes did the child have?"

"The child had only this pair of shoes and a pair of boots."

"When did you first suspect something had happened to the child?"

"In August, Mary Farley, showed me a piece of lilac print, also a piece of black yarn stocking. That was the 9th. Mary Farley lives next door to me."

"And what did you do with the pieces of clothing?"

"I gave the things given to me by Mary Farley to P.C. Taylor. The piece produced earlier are the same; they are in the state as when shown me when the little girl left, she had two pinafores of the same pattern as that produced, one in the bundle, and I put one out for her to put on. I put in two pairs of yarn stockings similar to the piece produced."

"When did you identify the body of the child?"

"I was shown the body of the child that was this month found, at the mine house. I knew it by the hair and clothes."

"How did you know by the hair and clothes?"

"The hair was cut short round by the ears. Mr. Jeffs showed me the clothes on the body; she had all those clothes on when I saw her last, except the chemise. I saw the chemise after it was taken off. I knew it; it was the same I had put in the bedroom the night before she left my house. The body had no boots on when I saw it. The boots produced I have seen before, they were Anna Maria Burgess's."

"Mrs. Marley, earlier, you recognised a Macintosh coat. How did you know it was the prisoner's?"

"The prisoner had a Macintosh while he lived with me and I saw it at the mine house. It was William Burgess's. I saw him wearing it on the 27th of July. The one produced is the same."

Karslake walked back to the table and looked at his notes quickly and then looked at Burgess, who was sitting calmly. He then turned back to Mrs. Marley and looked at her for a moment before asking, "In the ashes of the fire, found by Mr. Mills, there were hooks and eyes. How did you know that they were part of the child's clothing?"

"There were hooks and eyes about the dress of the little girl. I saw some burnt stuff that had been found in a heap. I picked up a piece of fur victorine myself, and gave it to P.C. Taylor. It is the same kind of fur at the tippet I put in the bundle and the fragments of print produced are the same as the print of which the pinafores were made."

Burgess watched her very anxiously during her examination, but remained silent.

Karslake sat down and looked at Mr. Rotton, who got up and cross-examined her, and asked, "In the time the prisoner stayed with you, did you witness any cruelty to the child?"

"No," she answered, "I did not see anything particular in his conduct. He did not seem very fond of the child, but I never saw him unkind to her, while he lodged with me."

"Do you know how much he was earning?"

"He was earning 2s a day and he paid me 1s a week for his own lodging."

"Do you know when he was married?"

"No. I do not know when he was married."

"What was his attitude when he was drinking?"

"He was very often in liquor, but he behaved very civil in the house. When he was in that state, he would come and take his meals and go straight to bed. I do not know what his conduct was out of the house."

"How long have you known the prisoner?"

"I have known him for about five years."

"Apart from the child, did you know any other person from the family? Father? Brother? Sister?"

"I did not know his father, or his brother and sister."

"You, as well as the other witnesses have mentioned the Macintosh coat and you all say it belonged to the prisoner. Can you tell the court how you know definitely that the Macintosh produced is the prisoners?"

"I know the Macintosh by his frequently wearing it and I know it, because the collar was lined with dark cloth and by his frequent wearing it."

"And you can recognise the piece of cloth as the child's, by how?"

"I know the bit of fur to be the same kind as the victorine."

"What was his attitude to the child?"

"During the time the prisoner lodged with me, he did not appear to be fond of the child, but I did not see any unkindness and he was a cheerful man generally."

Mr. Karslake stood up, when Mr. Rotton had finished and re-examined her. He asked, "When the prisoner left that fateful morning, he was wearing leggings. Do you know where they are now?"

"The legging's belonging to the Macintosh are at my house now."

"I see. And you say he always wore the Macintosh?"

"In the wet weather he used to wear the Macintosh and with the weather being as it is lately, I had ample means of seeing it."

"When was the last time you saw him wear the coat?"

"I did not see him wear it after the 27th of July, to the best of my knowledge."

"What time of the day did you usually see the prisoner?"

"He used to go to work about seven o'clock in the morning and leave work at six o'clock."

"Did the prisoner and the child spend much time together?"

Sarah shrugged her shoulders and replied, "I did not see him and the child much together while he was with me. He did not appear over fond of the child, but he was not cruel to her."

When Mr. Karslake finished questioning her, he told her to leave the box and sat down.

Karslake then stood up again and called William Cockram to the box.

"I am William Cockram," he said, "and I work on Exmoor, in the mines. In July last I lodged at Marley's cottage and Burgess lodged there too."

"Do you know where the prisoner worked?" Karslake asked.

"He worked at 'Picked Stones' taking off the deads, and I was working under ground. I was doing this the week before this happened."

"How long was the little girl staying at the cottage?"

"For three weeks the prisoner's little girl was lodging there, sleeping in the same bed with me and the prisoner."

"What happened on that last morning?"

"On Sunday 25th of July, Burgess turned out of bed. My watch was hanging up on the side of the bed. The prisoner took my watch down and asked me to tell him the time. I did, it was half-past-three. It was getting daylight. He said it was raining, and I said "You are not going to take away your little child now it's raining, so, are you Burgess?" He replied, "This is nothing." After he was dressed he said to the child, "Come Anna, turn out, we must be gone." The little girl got up, and left the room with him. I did not notice whether she was dressed. I went to sleep again."

"When did you see him again?"

"The same evening I saw the prisoner about nine o'clock. I was at church in the afternoon. I saw him when I went to bed."

"Do you know if he was working those last few days?"

"He continued to work until the Saturday proceeding the Tuesday, when he went away. On that day, Tuesday 10th of August, I saw him, when he told me he had been amongst friends hay harvesting. He worked as a day labourer."

"What can you tell me about the Macintosh coat?"

"I knew of his having a Macintosh."

"When was the last time you saw that coat?"

"I saw the Macintosh at the Wheal Eliza mine when the body was taken out. I knew it by the wear and the blue cloth on the collar. That was William Burgess's. I saw him with it on the Tuesday morning, I never saw it afterwards until I saw it at the mine."

Karslake sat down and after a moment, Mr. Rotton got up and asked, "You say you recognised the coat, how did you know it was the prisoner's?"

"The Macintosh was very much worn. I never saw one with a blue collar like that."

"How long have you known the prisoner?"

"I had known the prisoner for three years. His wife was living then. Prisoner was intimate with me while lodging at the Gallon House. I saw no difference in his manner. He did not seem to care about the loss of his wife; never saw any bad conduct of his towards the child."

"Did he say anything to you about the rent?"

Cockram paused and quickly looked at Burgess, then back at Rotton and replied, "He never complained to me about half-a-crown being too much for her keep."

"What was his drinking like?"

"Same as most men. He came in drunk sometimes."

Mr. Rotton sat down and before Karslake stood up, the judge asked, I understand that he had arranged to go the week before, what did the prisoner say?"

"He got up the Sunday before between six and seven and then said it was too late, I don't know whether the little child was sleeping there at the time."

The judge nodded, looked at Karslake, who shook his head and the judge told Cockram to step down.

Karslake called to the box, John Mills, who said, "I am the son of a farmer, near Gallon House cottage, Exmoor. On the 11th of August I was walking across my father's allotment; when I saw a spot in a corner where a fire had been made. I put my foot upon it and broke it in. Then I went to work. The next day my brother was with me; I went to the heap and told him something had been burnt there. I got a stick and turned the stuff about. I saw some buttons, hooks and eyes, and pieces of linen there. I did not pick them up and cannot swear to them."

Mary Farley was called next and in her testimony she said, "I am Mary Farley, and I live at the cottage next to Mrs. Marley's near the Gallon House. (I would like to point out at this moment, that she lied in her testimony, as on the 7th of December, thirteen days earlier, she married William Cockram at Exford.) On 15th of August I went to Mr. Mills' allotment. I had heard of the fire and went to the place. I turned the stuff over, and found a piece of black yarn stocking, and a piece of lilac print. I gave them to Mrs. Marley."

"Miss Farley," Karslake said, "did you know the prisoner before he moved into the cottage?"

"I had known the prisoner four or five months."

"Did you know about his drinking?"

"I did not know anything as to his getting drunk. I do not know how was to his getting drunk."

"Did you know how he treated his daughter?"

"I do not know how to the habit of treating his little girl."

With Mary's short testimony, she was asked to stand down and the next witness was called.

"My name is William Smith," the witness said, "I am a shoemaker, and keep a public house, at North Molton. I know the prisoner, and have known him since May last. In that month the prisoner came to my house to a club; and he afterwards gave me an order for a pair of boots for his child. A few days afterwards a woman named Ford brought a little girl six years old to be measured for a pair of boots. I measured her, made the boots, and sent them home by my son; I have not been paid for them."

Mr. Rotton asked, "You said that you made the boots, but you also said your son made them, which one of you made the boots?"

"My son made the boots in my shop," Smith replied.

"So you have seen the prisoner when he has been drinking?"

"Yes, I have seen the prisoner when he'd rather a drink at my house, and have seen him two or three times in liquor."

Smith stepped down from the box and John Moore took the stand.

"I am John Moore; I am a labourer, living at Porlock. I am married to the prisoner's sister, and live at West Porlock with her, and take care of her mother, who is bed-ridden. On the 25th of July on a Sunday morning, Burgess came to my house. He came in between seven and eight o'clock; it was a stormy morning, and he was very wet. I was in bed when he came. He stopped three-quarters of an hour altogether and had his breakfast. He brought nobody with him. I did not know his little girl; never saw her in my life. I had not seen him for three weeks or a month before that. He had made no arrangement at the time to bring his child to my house. About twelve months before, when his wife died, he had spoken to me to take his little girl; but instead, he let Mr. Steer have her at Exford. Burgess's wife died nearly two years ago. I never visited them at Honeymead farm. I know the two eldest children; one was about seventeen and the other fifteen."

Mr. Rotton asked him, "How long have you been married, Mr. Moore?"

"I have been married to the prisoner's sister about fifteen years."

"Do you know of any other family he has apart from his sister, your wife, his mother and remaining children?"

"Her father was dead at that time, he died before then."

"Anybody else?"

"I know two brothers of the prisoner. One is alive now. The other died in a lunatic asylum. I knew him."

"What do you know about his wife?"

"The prisoner's wife died about two years ago. Do not know whether they lived happily. I do not know whether he has been in the habit of drinking, but I did not often see him."

"At the time of the prisoner's wife's death did he approach you about the child?"

"He wanted to make some arrangements for me to take the child on his wife's death. We were willing to take it; but the prisoner did not come at the time appointed, but let Mr. Steer have the child in the meantime."

"Did you know where he worked?"

"I know the prisoner worked somewhere on the forest, but I did not know where."

"Apart from that Sunday morning, the prisoner never visited you any other time at the time of the child's disappearance?"

"I sometimes work half-a-mile or a mile from my house. A person might come there in my absence and I not know it."

"Did you and the prisoner ever come to blows?"

"I never had any quarrel with the prisoner. I was not afraid of him. He once asked me to go a little way with him on the road, and I did. The prisoner said "You are like the Withy pool men, carry a stick." I swear I did not carry it to protect myself from the prisoner, fearing he would make an attack upon me."

Mr. Rotton sat down and the judge asked the witness, "On that Sunday he visited you and your family are you sure about the time he got to your house?"

Moore looked at the judge and replied, "The prisoner might have been there on the Sunday morning before seven, but it was about that time he knocked on our door."

"How did he seem when you saw him?"

"He seemed cheerful and ate a good breakfast; we had bacon and bread and butter and coffee for breakfast."

The judge nodded and said, "Thank you, Mr. Moore, you may step down."

As he stood down, Karslake recalled Constable Taylor, and as he re-took the stand, Karslake asked, "Constable Taylor, as a police officer, you obviously know the area?"

Taylor replied, "Yes. I know Exmoor."

"How long have you known the prisoner?"

"I had known the prisoner about eighteen months."

"Do you know anything about his family?"

"I knew nothing about his family before that."

"Was the prisoner in your custody at Dulverton and what happened?"

"Yes. The prisoner was in my custody at Dulverton – he was handcuffed."

Burgess startled the court by standing up and shouting, "I wasn't handcuffed."

"He was handcuffed," Taylor said, "But, I took them off to give him his breakfast. While I was turning round, he took up a pair of scissors and knocked them into his throat, making a wound about two inches long and an inch deep. I found the scissors in front of him. I laid him on his back, and sent for a surgeon. As I held his hands, he tried to get his fingers to the wound to tear it open; and he told me if he could see the chance he would make away with himself. I sent for a surgeon, considering it quite necessary."

"Thank you. You may step down."

As Taylor left the box, the Judge said, "I think at this stage of the proceedings, I will adjourn the court for ten minutes." He then hit the bench with his gavel, stood up and left the courtroom.

The Wheal Eliza Murder

Chapter Sixteen

When the trial was resumed, Mr. Rotton addressed the jury for the defence. He said, "The court has taken care that the prisoner should have the benefit of a counsel to defend him; and I have undertaken that task. I should endeavour to place before them, in the best way that I possibly could, the facts that had been brought forward, so as to elicit from them whatever was favourable to the prisoner. I confess that the awful responsibility would have been too much for me, and even when I had undertaken it I should have shrunk from the task, were it not that I knew I had two powerful assistants in the court, his lordship and themselves. His lordship, because he felt certain that he would, as he had done, amply supply any deficiency that might arise, or any shortcomings on his part, by putting those questions to the witnesses which he, from inexperience, might neglect; and the jury, because it was the feeling of every class in England to take the side of the weaker, and I am sure that they would, with that feeling, regard the remarks that I've made, not so much with an eye, or rather he should say an ear, to the manner in which they were brought forward, as to their own value. I am convinced that there would be, on their parts, an indulgent attention, and they would look rather to the things said than to the speaker. I think that, the case being one in which they were called upon to rely so much on the minute points, there had been a great absence of precision in the facts that were produced, and those minute circumstances were wanting that ought to be brought forward to enable them to form a right judgment in a case so important as one in which the life of a fellow creature was concerned. It ought to be shown in evidence, not only in what manner the crime was committed, but what was the motive for committing it; supposing that it was an act of murder, the act of a man responsible at the moment for his conduct.

"Doubts on these points must have arisen in the course of the cross-examination. I might as well say at once that the points which he chiefly rested his defence, were the absence of any motive, the want of premeditation, and the monstrousness of the crime itself, and partly, also, the subsequent conduct of the prisoner; and I trusted on these points to be enable to raise such doubts as would save that man from the doom which otherwise awaited him. I had been in hopes that I should be able to bring evidence before the jury, to show the state of the prisoner's family; and this would have thrown additional light upon the subject on which I was addressing them. This I had been unable to do. The prisoner had been, all his life, a labouring man, and was unable to put very much into his purse, earning barely sufficient to keep himself and family: and he was unable to furnish himself with the means of defence. I was therefore unable to produce those witnesses; I could only endeavour to elicit something in the prisoner's favour out of the mouths of witnesses who came to prove his guilt, and not his innocence; and I could not expect to get much out of them, or that they would take much trouble, if any substantiate his innocence. It might be that, for the want of evidence, I should be unable to raise that reasonable doubt which would save this poor man's life; at all events, it would be much more satisfactory, both to myself and the jury, if the witnesses I had referred to could be called. It might enable him to substantiate the doubt I should endeavour to raise; or, if on the other hand, by the cross examination of the counsel for the Crown, those doubts should be set aside; it would still be a satisfaction that no effort had been left untried on the prisoner's behalf. With regard to those who had been examined, it appeared that the conduct of the prisoner towards the child was of a kind father. It was true, that among poor people there was not the same solicitude exhibited, and their feelings were not so acutely expressed, as was sometimes the case with other classes; but he thought the jury were justified, in forming the conclusion that the prisoner was fond of the child.

"A point that appeared to press against him was that of his objecting to pay the weekly sum of 2s 6d; there had been a great doubt thrown upon that. A question was put by his Lordship as to the time when that objection was made; and it appeared that, at the time he took the child and made the bargain, he attempted, and who would not? To get lowest terms he possibly could. If that was so, if the prisoner merely attempted then to get better terms, all motive for crime vanished for that was the only motive suggested. Taking this into consideration; and admitting as had been shown by several witnesses, that the prisoner was able to pay the money, considering also that he was usually fond of the child, did not the idea arise in their mind, from what cause could a crime so horrible, so atrocious, as had been attributed to the prisoner, have originated? It was attempted to be made out that he had killed a being, his own flesh and blood, to whom he never in his life exhibited the slightest unkindness, and to whom they might fairly presume, that he was attached; and what could suggest itself to their minds but that there was strange power working within him than had hitherto been suggested. I could imagine that the seeds of madness in him and of which perhaps he had never before shown the slightest symptoms broke out and led him to commit the deed with those circumstances of horror that had been referred to. This supposition was not at all inconsistent with the facts. The jury must be aware what power existed in madness; and that persons in that state, upon committing an act often took care to conceal it. It was possible, he maintained, that the feeling of madness having been evinced, after the commission of the deed, it calmed down, the prisoner might to a considerable extent, have recovered his reason: the desire of life would then strongly arise, that desire which was so natural to us all, as to be regarded as an instinct; belonging, perhaps rather to the animal than the intellectual nature; and this would account for all the subsequent acts relating to the concealment of the body. I could fancy that, reason having returned, the horror of the act would drive the wretched man, unable to bear the familiar scenes to which he was accustomed, from the place, like a second Cain, with the brand of God, not upon his brow, but in his heart, and lead him to seek amid new scenes and occupations, to get rid of the painful recollections of the horrible deed he had committed. The supposition was also consistent with the conduct of the prisoner when brought before the magistrate at Dulverton and the attempt which he made, with the greatest determination, upon his own life.

"Attempts of this character were the constant accompaniment of insanity; and the verdicts of coroner's juries were proving every day, that the act of self destruction might itself be regarded at one great proof of insanity. This determination of the prisoner to commit suicide had remained with him ever since; it seemed not to have deserted him for a moment; and he was obliged to be watched with the greatest care, to prevent his committing the act. Comparing this with the previous conduct of the prisoner towards the child, and the want of pre-meditation, it was a strong point in his favour. With regard to premeditation, it was true that Moore was called to show that the prisoner made no arrangement to leave the child with him; but Moore's wife was not called; and possibly the prisoner might have made the arrangement with his sister, and she might not have communicated it to her husband. At the moment he went out, he might, therefore, have been actually intending to take her with him to Porlock, and leave her there. The whole of these circumstances were consistent with the idea of madness suddenly arising in the prisoner's mind. I regret that I had not been able to bring evidence of the fact that madness had existed in the prisoner's family; but I had elicited from one of the witnesses, the suggestion that such was the fact. Putting all these things together, the prisoner's fondness of the child, the want of pre-meditation, the monstrousness of the crime itself, and the suggestion of insanity in the family, I ask you whether there was not, supposing the act to have been committed by the prisoner, a very grave doubt as to his being for the time responsible for his acts. My learned counsel has been able to raise any such doubt as that, I was convinced that the jury would do their duty, and acquit the prisoner. From my inability to bring witnesses, and my own want of experience, I ask the greater indulgence on their part; and I leave the matter in your hands, confident that you would give it all the attention necessary, and all that would be required to justify yourselves, if you felt compelled so to do, in bunging in the awful verdict of guilty."

The Judge then summed up, requesting the jury to dismiss from their minds everything they might have heard on the subject before, and to form their opinions only on the evidence brought before them: They must not convict the prisoner except upon satisfactory evidence; but the interests of society required that they should not acquit him if that evidence was satisfactory. The Judge then said that he did not think he should be doing his duty either to the public or the prisoner on that solemn occasion if he did not read through the whole of the evidence; and he proceeded at length to enter into the evidence, remarking upon those portions which bore more particularly on the prisoner's innocence or guilt. The learned counsel, he observed had fallen into an error, in assuming that there was any complaint on the part of the prisoner of the 2s 6d per week being too much for the child's maintenance after the arrangement was first come to with Mrs. Marley; he (the learned judge) had fallen into the same error, and he therefore put some questions to this witness, and from what she said it seemed the prisoner did not complain at all of the charge being too high for the keep of the child after the bargain was made; nor was there anything in what was said at that time to Mrs. Marley, but what might have been expected to have taken place in making an arrangement for keeping the child. That was two days after he had taken the child away, so that it did not appear that the prisoner bad at anytime complained of 2s 6d being too much. Still it might be that he thought it a burden; but they had no evidence to show that this was the motive which actuated the prisoner, or rendered it desirable to get rid of the child; and in this respect he was bound to say the prosecution had failed. But while he pointed out this fact as favourable to the prisoner, they would find from the same witness's evidence that the life-taking (he would not say murder) away of this child with its clothes, had been premeditated the week before. Now, if under the delusion that some one had injured him, a person took away; the life of a fellow creature, if he was in such a condition as to be able to tell right from wrong, that delusion would not excuse him from the criminal responsibility of such an act. A remarkable instance of this kind occurred some years ago. A noble peer somehow thought his steward had injured him, and under this delusion shot the steward dead, and it was held that the person who committed the act knew the difference between right and wrong, and that he was criminally responsible for the consequences. So in this case, the jury would have to be satisfied first, whether there was anything wrong in the state of the prisoner's mind, and if they were so satisfied they would then say whether in their judgment his faculties were in such a state that he did not know be was doing anything against the law of God and man. In reference to the evidence of the witness Cockram, his lordship said, his testimony was very important as showing that the prisoner called up his daughter and took her away at an early hour on the Sunday morning; he also identified the Macintosh in which the body was wrapped having then the prisoner wear it on the Tuesday after he took away the child. If the theory of the prosecution that the prisoner put the body in the shaft were well-founded, it was clear that it could not have been there so early as two days after the child was last seen alive, for when round it was enveloped in the Macintosh belonging to the prisoner, and he was proved to have worn it subsequent to the removal of the child from Mrs. Marley's; thus he must have been dealing with the dead body on two different occasions. This witness was the man who knew the prisoner well, who slept with him by night and worked with him by day; and he was bound to tell the jury that such a witness was a very proper person to form an opinion as to the state and habits of the prisoner. As to that Cockram had been asked questions, and he told them that the prisoner was not different in his manner from other people, and that, he saw nothing about him to show that he was labouring under any mental disorder. In commenting on the evidence of Skewes, the learned judge remarked upon the length of time which elapsed after the prisoner had been apprehended and the finding of the body, which was only accomplished at length by the proper authorities at very great expense. For two hundred years or more, said his lordship, it had been a settled point in all prosecutions for murder that the body of the person alleged lo be murdered should be found; therefore that it was not deemed necessary in a conviction for murder that there should be a finding of the body. One of the learned judges in the time of Charles I, or Charles II, illustrated the frequent injustice of this law, as cases had arisen in which persons had been con-demned and executed for murder, and afterwards the persons who were supposed to have been murdered made their appearance; and so after that period in prosecutions like those it was considered necessary before anybody could be put on their trial for murder that the body should be found. Referring to the fact that when the child was put out of the way the first night and the second night, it had on no Macintosh, he said it was a strong circumstance in the case as against the prisoner, that there was found in the vicinity a trench or grave, dug in the soil, just wide enough, and deep enough, and long enough, for burying the child; and from the nature of the soil found upon the body and the clothes when taken out of the shaft, it was not unreasonable to believe that the child was put into this temporary resting place for a time, that was until a favourable opportunity for finally disposing of it. Then again as to the time; they found the prisoner leaving the Gallon House, at half-past-three, on Sunday morning, where was he from half-past three until half-past seven, when seen at the house of his sister at Porlock, by the witness Moore? This time was not accounted for; it was fair to the prisoner to say that the witness however did not open the door for him; he did not know what time the prisoner arrived at the house, nor was he aware how long he might have been at the door when Moore's girl let him in. Glancing at the evidence of Mr. Supt. Jeffs, detailing the admissions of the prisoner when apprehended at Swansea, and charged with the murder, the judge said, it would be for the jury to weigh those statements with the prisoner's conduct, and consider how far they established his guilt. It had been suggested by the learned counsel, on behalf of the prisoner, that that was not the language of a sane man; on the other hand it was staled by the counsel for the Crown that it was precisely the language likely to be used by a sane man labouring-under the pangs of remorse for a dreadful crime he had committed. He (the learned judge) was then addressing twelve innocent men, who had never imbrued their hands in the blood of an innocent and unoffending fellow creature, and therefore they could not know what were the pangs of remorse which naturally attacked a man who had been guilty of an act like that. But taking the language and conduct of the prisoner, with other circumstances, into their grave and careful consideration, they would say whether they saw anything in the case to lead them to the conclusion that thin conduct was not the result of the pangs of remorse, such remorse as a man would feel who had been guilty of the murder of his own daughter. It had been suggested that the attempt on his own life was an indication of insanity in the prisoner. On this he would only observe that it was not by any means a common thing, when all the pleasures of life were gone forever, whether the course of justice was overtaking the acts of the guilty, or things were going against a person who had committed crime, for such attempts to be made, and so defeat the law in punishing the offender. They would see that in the statements made to the police officer by the prisoner, "It's all right; I did it, and must die for it, I would sooner die than live. I shall never be happy any more," were made at a time when he was competent to understand what he was about, in giving directions about his box, and the disposal of his money and clothes. Even if it were true, as had been suggested, that the prisoner's brother had been in a lunatic asylum, which would not affect the present case without satisfactory evidence to show something wrong in the prisoner's mental faculties at the time of the murder, supposing the jury were satisfied that he took away the life of the child. No! Nor if it had been so of the prisoner himself, that in the course of his life he had been in a lunatic asylum that would have but little weight in favour, unless there was evidence that he was of unsound mind at the period when the crime was committed. As to this, it was sufficient for him to tell them there was no evidence at all of any unsoundness of mind in any of the prisoner's family; and unsoundness of mind, so long as a man knew what he was doing was wrong, was no excuse for a man to escape the consequences of an atrocious crime. If they believed the evidence of the policeman, the prisoner had confessed his guilt, he knew that for that crime his life was about to be shortly taken by the law, and that would in some way account for the prisoner's attempt to take it himself, to save himself from the suspense and agony of the forms of the law and a painful and ignominious death. I need hardly say that when prisoners were under sentence of death, they were constantly watched day and night, or in all probability they would put an end to their existence. It would therefore be for them to say whether the prisoner's attempt on his life was at all consistent with the behaviour of a sane person under such circumstances, or that of a man striving to escape from the punishment of the law.

"One thing must have struck their minds in the course of that inquiry. That the poor child did not put an end to its own existence was quite clear; that the child was murdered by somebody was equally clear. Then arose the question who was the last person she was seen with? The father of the child. They had his misstatements after he returned to the cottage, as to what had been done with the child. "Are there many other children there?" Mrs. Marley asked.

"Yes, but she will not stay there long," was the prisoner's answer. Then there were his misstatements about the boots. These misstatements must be taken with all the surrounding circumstances, and the jury would upon looking at the whole facts, say whether the hypothesis of the prisoner's innocence was consistent with those statements. It was true nobody saw the blow struck which caused the death of the child; but in nine cases out of ten the actual commission of the crime of wilful murder was not witnessed by any human eye. They would in this case consider and not upon the conviction, if they were of that opinion, whether there was not strong evidence of guilt apart from the man's own confession; and having heard that confession, they would say whether any reasonable doubt remained on their minds. He (the learned judge) wished, from the bottom of his heart, he could say anything more in favour of the prisoner upon the case as presented to them. The responsibility rested with them and not upon himself to weigh that evidence. The question for the jury was, supposing the prisoner took away the child's life, what state of mind he was in? It was out for the prosecution to suggest that he was in a sound state of mind, but it was the duty of the learned counsel on the other side to show that, if he bad ever been of unsound mind, and not only so, but that he was at the time in such a slate of unsoundness of mind that he was incapable of knowing he was offending against the laws of God and man; and unless they were satisfied of that, they could not acquit him on the ground of insanity. There was no evidence whatever that he ever laboured under any symptoms of insanity; when drunk, his conduct was described to be violent, but much as the conduct of other people; and when sober, as was the case with other men generally, he was quiet, and there was nothing different in his behaviour to that of other men of his class. With respect to the attempt on his life, it was not to be taken as indicative of unsound mind, for it was always necessary in the case of a person in the situation in which the man at the bar now stood, that he should be carefully guarded to prevent any attempt at self-destruction. There was evidence of premeditation and preconcert in the ordering of the child's things to be got ready on the preceding Sunday, when it appeared the prisoner got up too late to carry out his intention. As to the concealment of the body, it was clear from the fact of the Macintosh being found on the child, the body rested somewhere for several days before being put into the shaft, as the prisoner was proved to have worn the Macintosh after the child was last seen with him, and that the resting place was afterwards changed. It would be observed the care that had been used in tying up the body in the prisoner's Macintosh, the cutting the rope in two and tying two knots, the putting of two heavy stones in the bag to more effectually to sink the body, and its final deposit in the shaft of the mine. Then they found immediately afterwards, the prisoner leaving the neighbourhood, going to Swansea and, working at the docks there and there he was apprehended when he confessed "he did it, and must die for it." Having concluded his remarks on the evidence, his lordship observed, it was true a man's life was precious, and must not be taken away on any mere supposition, or inconclusive evidence of guilt, but precious, also, in the audit of the law were the lives of those little unprotected children; and unless they had the protection of the law, they were in many instances deficient of all protection whatever. The interests of the prisoner required that the jury should give this case their most anxious attention and care are they pronounced an adverse verdict; on the other hand, the security of society also required, if they had no reasonable doubt of the prisoner's guilt, let the consequences be what they might, that they should say so by their verdict. Whatever might be their verdict, he asked them to give it conscientiously, if they should yield to fear on the one hand, or to compassion on the other, they might come to such a decision as would make them reflect upon themselves throughout the rest of their lives. "Let me ask you then," the learned judge concluded, to calmly consider the facts of the case, exercise a dispassionate judgment upon thorn; and may God direct you to a right verdict."

As the jury turned round to consult, the prisoner eyed them anxiously; and his flushed temples and compressed lips at this moment, clearly indicated the workings of his troubled mind. He did not, however, attempt any renewal of his violent behaviour in the dock.

The jury deliberated for about half-a-minute, and in reply to the Clerk of Arraigns, the foreman pronounced a verdict of "GUILTY."

The Clerk, Mr. Gurney, turned to the prisoner and said, "William Burgess, you have been indicted for the wilful murder of Anna Maria Burgess. Upon your arraignment, you have pleaded not guilty, and thereby for your trial put yourself upon your country, which country has found you guilty. Have you anything to say why the court should not award judgment against you to die according to law?"

Burgess stood up and said to the Clerk, "Thank you, sir."

The court was silent and the Judge placed the black cap on his head and in a solemn tone, said, "Prisoner at the bar, you have been convicted after a full examination of the facts, and I may say, a confession by yourself, of the crime of wilful murder. That poor child, when you led her out that night, supposed she was conducted by the hand of a father, and little dreamt that she was led by a murderer. The example which will be made of you cannot protect her; but I trust it will protect many more and teach all who may raise their hands against their fellow creatures, the value which the law acts upon human life, and the certain consequences of taking it away maliciously. The law of this land is, that "Who so sheddeth man's blood, by man shall his blood be shed." There is no hope of mercy for you in this world. The best advice that I can give you is, resign yourself confiding to the religious instruction which will be afforded you, for so, and so only can you expect to meet your fate with any degree of composure, or resignation, or hope. The sentence of the law upon you is that you be taken hence to the place from whence you came, and from thence on a day to be appointed, to the place of execution, that you be there hanged by the neck until you be dead and may the Lord have mercy upon your soul!"

The judge paused for a second or two, and then added, "And that your body be buried within the precincts of the prison."

The judge was visibly affected during the delivery of the sentence.

Burgess, being escorted by the guards, then left the dock without the slightest outward manifestation of feeling at his awful position and was led back to his cell.

Chapter Seventeen

As the crowd dispersed from the court, Reverend Thornton, who was among them, held back to speak to Mr. Oakley, the Governor of Taunton Gaol. Thornton had been subpoenaed, but wasn't called to give his testimony. It had been a long weekend for him, as he travelled up to Taunton on Saturday and was told the trial wouldn't be until the Monday morning. Because he had to conduct his duties on Sunday, he travelled all the way back to Simonsbath and came back to Taunton that morning.

"Sir," he said to Oakley, "I am Reverend Thornton of Simonsbath, and I would like, if possible to see William Burgess."

"Reverend!" Oakley replied, "The Taunton authorities never compelled a condemned man to see anyone unless he so wished."

"I know," answered Thornton, "But..."

"The prisoner is a desperate man and has nothing more to fear. And I know very well, who you were and being one of the people that put him here, I fear for your safety if you went to his cell."

"Sir! I would risk an attack, and again I request to see the prisoner."

"Very well, Reverend, but you have been warned."

Thornton followed the thirty-nine-year-old Oakley out of the court-room and waited in Oakley's office, while a warder went to Burgess's cell, with Thornton's card. When he came back the warder said, "Reverend! He will be glad to see you."

As Thornton got up, Oakley got up too, and was about to follow when Thornton turned and said, "Please. I would like to see him alone."

"I cannot allow that," Oakley said, "What if he attacks you..."

"Please, I can assure you. No harm will come to me. But please, I really need to be alone with him."

"Very well, but a guard stays outside the cell at all times."

"That will be fine," Thornton replied, turned and followed the warder.

The warder showed Thornton where to go and told him there was a guard in the cell with Burgess. Thornton thanked him and the warder turned around and walked back.

Footsteps could be heard walking down the corridor. In the cell, a guard sat casually in the corner by the slightly ajar door. Caressing his beard, he watched the prisoner facing the wall, looking out of the barred window.

The footsteps stopped. The guard sat up straight. The door opened and Reverend Thornton looked at the prisoner.

"Good morning, Will," Thornton said.

Burgess turned to him; on his neck was a wide, recently-healed scar, he looked at Thornton and then turned back to the wall.

Thornton looked at the guard.

"Leave us for a moment," Thornton said.

The guard looked at the Reverend and then at Burgess.

"I will be alright," Thornton assured him.

"I will be just outside," replied the guard.

The guard left the cell, but left the door ajar and paced the corridor. Burgess stood with his back to the reverend, leaning his arm on the wall, hiding his face.

"You see before you a man guilty of his crime," Burgess said.

Thornton took off his cloak, sat down and said, "Why did you do it, Will? What made you kill your daughter?"

"I murdered my child for the purpose of saving 2s. 6d. per week that I might be enabled thereby to indulge myself in more drink; and to indulge in drunkenness I committed the awful deed."

Thornton looked at Burgess in disbelief.

"I dug a grave," Burgess continued, as he knelt in front of Thornton, "On that Sunday morning, immediately after I ki ... killed her. She was lying there, so peaceful. It pains me for what I done and I want to die."

Thornton rested his hands on Burgess and prayed for forgiveness for this man kneeling in front of him. And for a couple of hours they talked as Thornton gave Burgess spiritual advice and assistance. Burgess manifested some anxiety about the disposal of a few things, and gave direction to Thornton as to the application of his best clothes, if permitted by the authorities.

As Thornton was about to get up to go, Burgess turned and looked at Thornton, and said, "I want to see my other children. I love that Jane, almost as much as the one I killed."

"I will see what I can do to help you, but I would imagine that after killing one of your children, I hardly expect another young child to be very willing to visit you."

Burgess sat on his bed and began to cry. Sobbing, Burgess said, "My children have deserted me. I want to die."

Thornton got up and said, "Will, I will do my best to comply with your wishes, but I would like you to do something for me."

Burgess nodded.

Putting on his cloak, Thornton said, "I want you to listen to the Chaplain of the gaol."

"I promise."

Thornton turned to leave the cell and Burgess stood up and said, "I'd like to shake hands with you."

Thornton turned back and held out his hand.

Taking hold of Thornton's hand, Burgess said, "You hunted me, but you're a real friend."

Letting go of Thornton's hand, Burgess added, "To you, sir, go back to Simonsbath, and tell the drunkards there to forsake drunkenness and strong drinks, or they may yet stand a condemned felon, as I now stand."

"I will tell them, William, and I would, if you like, to visit you again?"

"Yes sir, I would like that," Burgess answered.

"And I will see your other children and if I can get them to come with me to see you."

"I will be forever grateful, sir, if you can."

Burgess shook Thornton by the hand again and when he let go, Thornton turned once more and left the cell. The prison guard re-entered the cell and sat back down in the chair and continued to watch Burgess. As Thornton started to walk down the corridor, he heard Burgess sobbing in his cell.

Thornton left the gaol and rode back to Simonsbath. Over dinner, he told his wife, Grace, what had happened and what he needed to do and when he finished dinner, he mounted his horse and rode Brimsworthy Farm in North Molton. When he got there, he was greeted by Burgess's children and then by forty-one-year-old John Hayes, son and relative of the Hayes from Withypool, where Burgess, in revenge, burnt down the farm.

As John Hayes reached Thornton, the Reverend said to the children, "I need to talk to Mr. Hayes, on very important business, now you run along and I will talk to you shortly."

As the children ran off, Thornton looked at Hayes, who nodded, then turned and walked back into the house. As Thornton followed, he watched the children play.

Once inside, John silently pointed to a chair and Thornton sat down.

"I need to talk to you about the children, John," Thornton said.

"What about them," Hayes replied.

"I've just come from Taunton and the trial."

"And I hope they found him guilty and their go'in to ang im."

"Yes they did. But that's not what I'm here for," Thornton said.

"Go on."

"I have spoken to Will Burgess."

"And?"

"He wishes to see his children before he dies, especially Jane."

"They know nothing about what he's done, we haven't told them."

"They are his children, their only parent."

"On your head be it, sir. You can ask them, but I won't assist you into talking them into going."

Thornton nodded and sent for Charles. When he arrived, Thornton sat him down and said, "Charles, I have some bad news for you, but you need to be strong."

The child nodded and Thornton said, "Charles, your little sister Anna is dead. She was murdered and your father is going to be hanged."

Charles stared at Thornton in disbelief.

"Did you know that your sister was dead?"

"Did father kill her?" was Charles's startling response.

"Well, yes, Charles, he did," Thornton replied.

"I always thought father would kill Anna Maria."

"Charles! Your father is in gaol and is going to be hanged and he wants to see you."

"I won't go, I don't care for he..., he killed my sister," sobbed Charles.

Thornton called for Jane and when he told her, what he had just told Charles,

Jane's reaction was the same. They both regarded their own murder by their father as a probable contingency.

Thornton promised them safety and told them that he would send them to and bring them back from Taunton, and that in after years, they would be sorry if they didn't go. After a while they agreed and after obtaining John Hayes' consent, Thornton got up, went outside, mounted his horse and galloped back to Simonsbath.

The next morning, Thornton sent his long suffering coach horse to North Molton, picked up the children and sent them with William Vellecott to Mr. Oakley's care.

Burgess saw them and as he hugged them, he cried and as Oakley kept watch the whole time, the children were quiet and scared. When they left, they could here their father crying all the way down the corridor. When they reached the end of the corridor, Charles turned around and with tear's rolling down his face, said gently, "I do love you, father." He turned around and Oakley led them out to Vellecott, who took them home.

For the next sixteen days, Thornton visited him a couple of times and in between had visits from thirty-four-year-old Reverend Frederick Howse, the gaol's chaplain, to whom he had promised Thornton to listen, if he saw his children. Burgess repeatedly acknowledged his guilt and the justice of his sentence; and he made similar admissions to the Reverend William R. Clark, a twenty-nine-year-old curate of St. Mary Magdalene, Taunton, who, at the request of the prisoner and the chaplain, kindly paid him pastoral visits on Tuesday, Wednesday, and Thursdays. Mr. Clark is of the opinion that Burgess was quite penitent, and he is said to have expressed a hope of salvation through the atoning blood of Christ. The chaplain, however, did not deem the culprit a fit person to receive the Holy Sacrament, and its administration was accordingly, dispensed with. Up to the very morning of his execution, Burgess continued to express a desire to destroy himself, and, having made one attempt upon his life before his committal, he was perpetually watched, to prevent the possibility of his committing suicide.

As he slept in his cell on his last night on Earth, Burgess tossed and turned in his sleep. A couple of times the guard looked in on him, as he heard Burgess call his dead daughter's name, but as he could see that he was asleep he moved back to his chair in the hallway and sat down.

"Anna! Anna!" Burgess called in his sleep and with his eyes shut he struggled with himself.

"Anna, Come here, child."

Anna moved closer to Burgess. He hugged her and said, "I do love you. You do know that, don't you?"

"Yes, Father," she said, wrapping her arms around his neck.

Burgess released her, placed his hands on her shoulders and looked into her eyes. He saw Anna smile at him. Burgess smiled back, "Come on let's go."

Anna turned and walked on. Burgess watched her walk off and as he started to stand up; he saw a big stick lying on the ground. He picked it up, stood up and walked after Anna, using the stick as a walking cane.

As he caught up with her, he said to her, "I love you. But I'm sorry."

Without turning round, Anna replied, "What for?"

Burgess swung the stick and hit her hard on the right side of her head.

Anna's body went limp and as she slumped, Burgess dropped the stick, grabbed her, and lay her softly down on the ground. He looked closer at her and noticed she was still breathing. He placed a hand on her chest and pushed down and with his other hand, placed it over her mouth, pinching her nose with his index finger and thumb. Within seconds, Anna Maria Burgess stopped breathing.

"Anna!" he shouted so loudly that the guard outside his cell nearly fell off the chair.

Picking himself up quickly and rushing to the cell door, he looked in and saw Burgess sitting on his bunk with his head in his hands, crying.

The guard opened the door. "Are you alright, Burgess?" he asked.

Burgess looked up. With tears running down his face, he replied sobbingly, "Yes. I just had a nightmare."

The guard looked at the pitiful sight before him and said, "I know it would be hard to do, but try and get some sleep. You'll need all your strength in the morning."

Burgess looked at him, nodded and lay down again. The guard watched for a few moments and then stepped back out of the cell, shut and locked the door. He straightened his chair and sat down, listening for any sound coming from inside the room. When he heard nothing, he reclined in the seat and relaxed.

Inside the room, Burgess tried to shut his eyes but couldn't, for the thought of seeing Anna's face again haunted him. Yet, in due time – what seemed a lifetime of struggling to keep them open – they slowly closed and he was a sleep.

He looked down at her lifeless body, lying in the mud, the rain hitting her face. He caressed her face and said, "I'm sorry, little maid. Your mother will look after you now."

With his bare hands, he dug at the wet mud. When the hole was big enough, he picked up Anna's body and placed it gently into the hole. Tears ran down his face as he caressed her cheeks once more. He wiped his face and started to spread the mud back over her body. When he was done, he picked up her belongings and walked off into the night.

On the morning of Friday 7th of January 1859, Burgess arose from his bed. He glanced over at the open door and saw the guard sitting on a chair half asleep. Burgess walked over to the bowl, picked up a jug and poured some water into it. He looked into the mirror; his eyes were red, and his face was pale. He hadn't slept much during the night; he had thrown himself onto his bed at the usual time with his clothes still on. He had spent most of the night very restless and when he did fall asleep it wasn't for long, as he tossed and turned. He woke with a start and stared at the wall for a few minutes and then lay back down and tried to get to sleep.

After dousing his face with cold water, he looked into the bowl. The droplets of water fell from his face and fell into the clear, cool water. As he stared at the water, a vision appeared from the bottom of the bowl of the lifeless body of Anna, as he threw her corpse down the dark mineshaft. He jumped back and stared at the bowl as the guard stood up. Burgess turned to the door and the guard raised his hand to his temple. And at a few minutes after six o'clock, Mr. Oakley, the governor of the prison appeared at the door.

"Morning, Burgess," he said, as he entered the cell.

Burgess nodded and walked back to his bed; he sat on it and looked up at the Governor.

"Good Morning, sir," Burgess answered.

"Did you get any sleep last night?"

"No, sir. As if being hanged isn't punishment enough, I am being punished as I sleep or try to."

"I know how you feel. I've had a few sleepless nights in my time."

"You would have thought that my last night on this earth, the good Lord, would have let me sleep."

"Well, the chaplain will be here shortly, maybe after he goes; you can catch up on a little sleep?"

"No, sir. When this is all over I will have plenty of time to sleep."

Oakley took out his pocket watch, looked at it and said, "Well, I will leave you to it and I will see you in a couple of hours."

"Thank you, sir," Burgess answered.

Shortly after Oakley had gone the Chaplain arrived. Two or three times during the morning, while in his cell, Burgess was found on his knees, apparently in prayer.

He partook of breakfast, consisting of the ordinary prison fare, and ate it tolerably well. Burgess was taken to the chapel a little after eight o'clock, where the usual service was performed in the presence of the other prisoners in the gaol. At the close of the service, Burgess was received by fifty-eight-year-old, William Calcraft.

Calcraft was a famous man in his own right as England's public executioner, from 1829 to 1874. He performed between four-hundred-and-fifty and five-hundred executions, including at least thirty-five women.

He was famous for his "short drops" which caused most of his clients to strangle to death. Entitled to keep the clothing and personal effects of the condemned, he sold them to Madame Tussaud for her waxworks and made a handsome profit. The dark-haired and white bearded man met Burgess at the chapel-door, and, as a precaution against apprehended violence on the part of the condemned, he was here subjected to the process of pinioning. He submitted to the operation calmly, and without visible emotion. A minute or two before the prison clock struck nine; the procession marched across the court yard to the steps leading to the drop. Burgess was preceded by Mr. Henry Sully, the forty-year-old, head turnkey, and immediately after him came the Reverend Clark, reading the offices for the burial of the dead, followed by the hangman. On getting towards the top of the steps to the leads, Burgess staggered slightly, but in other respects he seemed exceedingly firm and collected. He wore the same clothes as he did at his trial, having that morning changed the prison dress for his own. On being placed under the fatal beam, Burgess looked pale and haggard in the extreme. Calcraft speedily drew a white cap over Burgess's face and adjusted the cord round his neck with one end fasted to the beam above, and as the clock struck nine o'clock, he pulled the lever and instantly the drop fell. Burgess seemed to struggle a good deal, but in about a minute he had ceased to exist. He was a stout, well-built man. The body, after hanging an hour, was cut down and placed in a shell with the clothes on, and in the course of the morning it was interred within the gaol precincts pursuant to the judge's sentence! The crowd assembled on the occasion was much smaller than usual, many of the persons having evidently come from a distance.

The Wheal Eliza Murder

After witnessing the hanging, Thornton got on his horse, rode through the town and made his way to North Molton, at Brinsworthy Farm. When Thornton arrived, Charles and Jane came out to him. He put his arms around them, leading them back indoors and told them what had happened.

Thus ended the last sad scene of the Exmoor Forest Murder.

THE END.

About The Author

C.R. Woollands was born, raised and still lives in Oxford, England. He is married with three children. Following an accident at work in 2005, Clive has been wheelchair bound.

Not wanting to sink into despair at the hands of self-pity, he returned to his writing and research for his books. This research drives him to the areas where his tales take place; he meets with the people of the town and villages to build the characters of each story he writes.

He is a writer of different genres, but enjoys writing horror and mystery novels mostly.

Clive began writing on a whim – just after the birth of his first son – eighteen years ago. At the time, he wrote an autobiography, which he thought would be of interest to the child when he grew up.

This first writing was a departure point for Clive. A few years later he wrote his first novel, *Never Say Die*, a thriller set in the West Country of the UK. While writing this story, he realized he knew very little about writing a book. In time, he learned all of the tricks and rules and set out to write *Blood Moon* – a horror-mystery novel, which was published in 2010 under Clive's pen name, Robert H. Tempest. The story is set in the Norfolk Broads, and has attracted the readers from England and abroad.

While Clive writes mainly horror under the name of Robert H. Tempest, he uses his real name to write true crime and mysteries, such as *The Wheal Eliza Murder*.

CPSIA information can be obtained at www.ICGtesting.com
Printed in the USA
BVOW07s1043230614

357117BV00001B/219/P